A HARD DECISION

A HARD DECISION

WESTLEY THOMAS

Author's Tranquility Press
ATLANTA, GEORGIA

Westley Thomas / Author's Tranquility Press
3900 N Commerce Dr. Suite 300 #1255
Atlanta, GA 30344
www.authorstranquilitypress.com

Ordering Information:
Quantity sales. Special discounts are available on quantity purchases by corporations, associations, and others. For details, contact the "Special Sales Department" at the address above.

Any people depicted in stock imagery provided by Getty Images are models, and such images are being used for illustrative purposes only.
Certain stock imagery © Getty Images.

Because of the dynamic nature of the Internet, any web addresses or links contained in this book may have changed since publication and may no longer be valid. The views expressed in this work are solely those of the author and do not necessarily reflect the views of the publisher, and the publisher hereby disclaims any responsibility for them.

A Hard Decision / Westley Thomas
Hardback: 978-1-964037-13-4
Paperback: 978-1-964037-88-2
eBook: 978-1-964037-14-1

More praise for A Hard Decision

"This is a powerful story where the consequences of war are laid bare, as is the power of love and family."
RECOMMENDED by the US Review

"A highly-praised play that will leave you longing for more from the author."
Pacific Book Review

"A Hard Decision is a heartfelt and earnest exploration of complex emotional landscapes shaped by war. Its strength lies in its character-driven dialogue, making it an engaging read and potentially an even more compelling theatrical experience, allowing the audience to fully appreciate the gravity of the characters' words and experiences."
Literary Titan

"A powerful exploration of love, tough choices and how war affects people."
eBookFairs Book Awards

"Westley Thomas's play, A Hard Decision, focuses on the aftermath of war in a thought-provoking way. This should appeal especially to the friends and families of veterans, particularly where it considers the impact that war has on families and communities."
Foreword Review

"Thomas has found an intriguing premise and setting for A Hard Decision."
BlueInk Review

This book is a recipient of the following prestigious book awards:

Pacific Book Review Notable Book
2023 Book of the Year Awards, Action/Adventure category
2023 Firebird Book Awards, Current Events category
2023 American Writing Awards, Legacy-Fiction category
2023 Titan Book Award, Military category
2023 Paris Book Festival, General Fiction
2023 Indies Today Awards, Romance category
2024 Great Southwest Book Festival Awards, Fiction category
2024 Southern California Book Festival, Fiction Literary category
2024 eBookFairs Awards, Suspense category

This book is dedicated to my wife Yvonne P. Parker Curry-Thomas. I thank God for her love and support and standing with me giving guidance, encouragement, and inspiration in all my dreams, goals, and ambitions, along with her superb effort editing A Hard Decision. To all my Veteran Brothers and Sisters who have served in the U.S. Military, and to my Marine Corps buddies you are my Family Forever.

ONCE A MARINE ALWAYS A MARINE.

SEMPER FI! OORAH!

THE MAIN CHARACTERS

WILLIAM DICKENSON
ZERA DICKENSON
STEVE ROGERS
JAHAD ROGERS
MARGARITE BROWN
LILLIAN BROWN

CHARACTERS IN ORDER OF APPEARANCE

WILLIAM DICKENSON, husband of Zera
ZERA DICKENSON, wife of William
VC/INTERROGATOR, enemy
VC/SOLDIER #1, enemy
BONG, Viet Cong traitor
VC/SOLDIER #2, enemy
CAPTAIN STEVE ROGERS, POW (Prisoner of War)
AIR FORCE REPRESENTATIVE #1
AIR FORCE REPRESENTATIVE #2
MARGARITE, Zera's long-time girlfriend
REVEREND FORREST MITCHELL,
(Senior Pastor of Faith Tabernacle Baptist Church)
MARINE, POW (Prisoner of War)
JAHAD, son of Steve and Zera
LILLIAN, daughter of Margarite
BARBARA HERSHEY, friend of Zera and Margarite
MILDRED ANSON, friend of Zera and Margarite
NEWSPAPER MAN, owner of news stand
WEASEL, mugger
MONKEY, mugger
JOSH, mugger
NATE, mugger
JULIO, mugger
POLICE OFFICER
JAMES HUDD, Assistant Pastor of Faith Tabernacle Baptist Church
ROBERT BROWN, ex-husband of Margarite

ACT I

The action of the play takes place during and after the Vietnam War era, on Staten Island in the North Shore Area.

Anyone visiting from the other boroughs wouldn't believe Staten Island to be part of New York City because of the likeness it has to the suburbs and the fact it is surrounded by water, New Jersey, Brooklyn, and Manhattan.

Families were families always sitting down to the dinner table to enjoy meals together. Everyone on the Island knew each family in their neighborhood. Families socialized at church, the beaches, school, bus and boat rides, parties, special events, picnics in the parks, and especially on Friday and Saturday nights, at card parties and places selling chicken and fish dinners.

A historical event is about to take place causing a complete change that will create a heavy impact on American families, for which many were not prepared.

Young men average ages nineteen to twenty-six, will be shipped off to war in Vietnam, in Southeast Asia.

There are many stories to be told and chapters still to be written. Besides friendship this play surrounds the love of two childhood sweethearts, William and Zera.

SCENE I

WILLIAM AND ZERA, MARRIED AFTER GRADUATING FROM HIGH SCHOOL, HAVE RETURNED FROM THEIR HONEYMOON.

WILLIAM: *(opening the door)* I know it's not much but this is our new apartment.

ZERA: *(standing in the doorway smiling gleefully)* William, it's beautiful!

WILLIAM: *(blocks doorway with his arms)* Wait a minute, Zera, it has to be done the right way.

ZERA: *(dazed)* What, William?

WILLIAM: Just stand back and let me carry the bags in first. I'll come back for you. I have to carry you across the threshold. *(hurrying, he takes the bags inside and returns for Zera)* See, that didn't take long.

ZERA: You didn't have to come back for me, I could have walked in.

WILLIAM: No, Zera, letting you walk in will bring bad luck.

ZERA: Are you sure you can handle me and our expected addition to the family?

WILLIAM: Sure I can, *(carrying her inside, he quickly puts her down)* now how was that?

ZERA: That was too fast, you didn't carry me far enough!

WILLIAM: The threshold is from out there to here. *(he demonstrates to her by stepping out into the hall and back into the apartment)* See, it's not far.

ZERA: So I noticed.

WILLIAM: Zera, come on, let's sit down and relax for a minute on the sofa. Can I get you anything?

ZERA: Yes, you can.

WILLIAM: What?

ZERA: I have a craving for pickles.

WILLIAM: *(aloud)* Pickles! *(William laughs)* pickles, pickles! Are you kidding, Zera, at this time of the night?

ZERA: Well, what's so funny about craving for pickles? I'm expecting, don't you remember?

WILLIAM: Of course I remember, but we don't have any pickles in the apartment. I'll go to the store right now and buy some.

ZERA: You don't have to go now, it's late, I can wait until tomorrow. Give me a kiss. *(they kiss and she takes William's hand and places it on her stomach)* Do you feel that?

WILLIAM: *(looking at Zera)* I don't feel anything.

ZERA: It's the baby. It's moving. *(looking into William's eyes)* William our honeymoon at Atlantic City was really beautiful.

WILLIAM: Zera, this is the one day I longed for, ever since eighth grade. I always hoped that you would be my wife and we would spend a happy life together raising our children.

ZERA: But, how can we, William? You have to go fight in that stupid, stinking war. *(hugging William)* I really wish you didn't have to go. I'm afraid, *(rubs her hands together)* I'm afraid you might get hurt, killed, or come back crippled.

WILLIAM: *(with assurance)* Everything will be alright, you'll see.

ZERA: *(speaking in a girlish voice)* You promise, do you really promise?

WILLIAM: I promise, *(crossing his heart)* I cross my heart!

ZERA: William, I love you.

William: *(he kisses her)* I love you too, Zera. *(they stand up)* You know something? Right now, I feel like the happiest man in the world.

ZERA: William, when you leave next week to join your Air Force comrades over in Vietnam, will you be thinking about me?

WILLIAM: *(holding her shoulders)* You know I will, Zera. I'll write to you every day.

ZERA: What about the baby? Have you chosen a name?

WILLIAM: *(smiling)* Yes, I have chosen two names.

ZERA: *(enthused)* You did?

WILLIAM: Zera, if the baby is a boy, I want you to name him Tayari or "T" for short.

ZERA: *(looking at William)* That's beautiful, and what about the girl?

WILLIAM: If it's a girl, we'll call her Ti'Isha or Mariah.

ZERA: Those names are so beautiful, I love them all. I can't wait.

WILLIAM: And I love you, my proud and expecting lovely wife. *(they embrace)*

———

FADE OUT

<u>SCENE</u> II

THE LETTER

ZERA, AT HOME, READS LETTER FROM WILLIAM. HE IS IN VIETNAM. SHE IS WORRIED BECAUSE IT HAS BEEN A LONG TIME SINCE LAST HEARING FROM HIM.

ZERA: *(reading William's letter)*

Hello Love,

I miss you and I hope you're doing well awaiting our bundle of joy. Give my love and regards to the family and our dearest friends. I did promise you I would write every day. If you don't hear from me for awhile, don't worry. I'll be okay and drop you a line as soon as I can.

We're about to step up our air operations because we've been constantly on red alert. "Charlie's" been dumping barrages on the air base pounding us morning, noon and night. Marble Mountain was hit last week and the perimeter at China Beach was stepped up to prevent Sampan Sniper Teams from coming ashore.

The barrages were hot last night. This place lit up like a Christmas tree. Our Commander called in the Marines from Marine Headquarters Group One Reactionary Force. They formed a perimeter around the air strip, in the event that "Charlie" would attempt to overrun the base. "Charlie" is a shrewd operator and will desperately do anything to take out our aircraft so we must constantly be on our P's and Q's.

Well, Love, I'll close for now. Love always and forever.

Your husband,
William

—————

FADE OUT

<u>SCENE III</u>

DURING A MISSION OVER THE HAIPHONG AREA, CAPTAIN STEVE ROGERS AIRCRAFT WAS SHOT DOWN AND HE WAS CAPTURED BY THE (VC) VIET CONG. ROGERS AS A CAPTURED PRISONER OF WAR, IS AIDED IN HIS ATTEMPTED ESCAPE BY A (VC) VIET CONG TRAITOR.

VC/INTERROGATOR: Soldiers, bring in the traitor Bong. *(VC/ Soldier #1, pushes the Viet Cong traitor into the interrogation room)* Bong, so it was you that aided Captain Steve Rogers in his attempted escapes. What do you say for yourself? *(pause)* So you have nothing to say, huh? Soldier, bring in the next prisoner.

VC/SOLDIER #2: *(agitated forcefully pushing prisoner Captain Steve Rogers into the interrogation room, he is blindfolded, hands tied, dragging his feet trying to walk)* I said, move! You're not moving fast enough, move!

VC/INTERROGATOR: So it is you again, Captain Steve Rogers. Aren't you tired of trying to escape?

CAPTAIN ROGERS: *(very arrogant)* What's it to you? You're nothing but a bunch of Viet Cong assholes.

VC/SOLDIER #2: *(grabs Rogers in the face)* You call us assholes? Shut up your filthy mouth before I show you how we treat asshole prisoners like you. You Americans are a bunch of fools.

VC/INTERROGATOR: Captain, do you know what we do to traitors?

VC/SOLDIER #2: *(agitated, poking Rogers, and pushing him into the chair because he does not respond)* Speak when you are spoken to, don't you hear the interrogator talking to you?

VC/INTERROGATOR: *(angrily demanding)* Who was it this time that helped you attempt your escape? Was it that Marine? If it was, he will be in for a rude awakening. Don't you fools know you can't escape our prison grounds?

VC/SOLDIER #2: *(arrogant, loud, shaking his fist and poking Rogers)* You Americans don't learn very well. This is a war you'll never win.

VC/INTERROGATOR: Captain Rogers! I ask you again, what was the purpose of your mission?

CAPTAIN ROGERS: I told you the purpose already! How many times do I have to repeat myself?

VC/INTERROGATOR: *(angered and intimidated by answer)* You gave the wrong answer, Captain. I demand to know the purpose of your mission?

CAPTAIN ROGERS: To kill Gooks! You assholes!

VC/SOLDIER #2: I told you to shut up your filthy mouth.

VC/INTERROGATOR: Get this prisoner out of my face, his days are numbered.

FADE OUT

<u>SCENE IV</u>

AFTER ESCAPING THE PRISON COMPOUND CAPTAIN ROGERS IS HIDING IN THE BUSH WITH BONG WHO IS PLANNING AN ESCAPE ROUTE.

BONG: Captain Rogers the escape route has been set, contact has been made with those who will help you get back to your American installation.

CAPTAIN ROGERS: Thank you, Bong. I am very grateful for all your help.

BONG: I wish you well, Captain Rogers. I just want you to know that your escape means my death. If you make it back to your side across American lines, then I and my family can rest in peace. I was forced to fight this war and I am tired of all this killing. *(they depart running in opposite directions)*

FADE OUT

LIGHTS UP

AFTER BEING CAPTURED BY THE VC/SOLDIERS, BONG AND CAPTAIN ROGERS ARE BROUGHT BACK TO THE PRISON COMPOUND, THE INTERROGATOR IS OUTRAGED.

VC/INTERROGATOR: Soldiers, please bring in the traitor Bong and Captain Rogers. *(they enter)* Captain Rogers I have someone here that you might recognize. *(pause)* Soldier, remove the Captain's blindfold. Captain Rogers, this is Bong, the traitor. He continues to go against us to help Americans escape. We want you to see what happens to traitors. Bong what do you have to say now, Bong? You still have nothing to say? Huh! Bong here's a weapon, if you are not a traitor, shoot Captain Rogers. All you have to do is pull the trigger, shoot the Captain and we'll let you go. *(Bong takes the weapon. Pondering, he holds it in his hand)*

FADE OUT / *(sound of gunshot)*

SCENE V

THE MISSION

WILLIAM'S AIR RECONNAISSANCE MISSION IS UNDER A HEAVY CONCENTRATION OF ENEMY ANTI-AIRCRAFT FIRE. HIS AIRCRAFT IS SEVERELY HIT.

WILLIAM: Mayday! Mayday! Red Leader! Red Leader! This is Dickenson, I've been hit. I'm losing cabin pressure, I'm losing altitude. My gauges are going haywire, the heat and smoke are building up inside my cabin. I'm going down. Over and out! *(He ejects and descends, his feet touch the ground and he is surrounded by Viet Cong.)*

VC/SOLDIERS: *(yelling out)* Dun Li! Dun Li!

FADE OUT

<u>SCENE VI</u>

TWO MEN IN MILITARY UNIFORM COME TO ZERA'S APARTMENT.

ZERA: *(doorbell rings)* Who is it?

AIR FORCE REPRESENTATIVE #1: We are looking for a Mrs. Zera Dickenson.

ZERA: Just a moment please, *(she opens the door)* yes I'm Mrs. Zera Dickenson, who are you?

AIR FORCE REPRESENTATIVE #1: We are Representatives from the Air Force Casualty Services. *(extending the envelope)* We are here, Ma'am to present you with this envelope, and to inform you . . .

ZERA: *(interrupting, takes the envelope)* What is this? Is this about my husband?

AIR FORCE REPRESENTATIVE #2: Yes it is Ma'am. We have been asked to inform you of the tragic loss of Captain William Dickenson. Details and information are enclosed inside the envelope.

ZERA: No! No! No! William! William! William! Oh no, not my William!

AIR FORCE REPRESENTATIVE #1: We are very sorry Ma'am for the loss of your husband, we extend to you and your family our condolences.

ZERA: Thank you, Sir. *(they leave, she closes the door and sits down to open the envelope, she breaks down crying)* No! No! No! William! William! William! Oh! No! Not my William, my baby, my baby, my baby, my baby! *(yelling)* William! William! I love you, I love you.

FADE OUT

<u>SCENE VII</u>

MARGARITE IS AT THE HOME OF HER BEST FRIEND ZERA. THEY ARE AWAITING THE LIMOUSINE TO GO TO WILLIAM'S FUNERAL SERVICE.

MARGARITE: I'm so sorry, Zera! I can feel the pain and hurt you're going through. I can imagine how unbearable your pain must be and your love for William. We know God will make your pain go away and take away your sorrow.

ZERA: Margarite, I don't know what I'd do if it weren't for your support. I know I wouldn't be able to make it alone.

MARGARITE: That's why I'm here, girl. You can count on me at any time, that's what friends are for.

ZERA: *(nervous)* I'm afraid. Margarite, I don't feel right. My William is gone, my William is gone. How will I make it without him? He'll never see his baby I'm carrying. I don't know if I can take going to William's funeral.

MARGARITE: *(doorbell rings, Margarite opens door)* Zera, the limousine is here. Are you ready? We have to go.

———

FADE OUT

SCENE VIII

FUNERAL SERVICE CONDUCTED BY REVEREND FORREST MITCHELL (SERVICE BEGINS WITH CONGREGATION SINGING, READING OF SCRIPTURES, AND TESTIMONIALS BY FAMILY AND FRIENDS)

REVEREND MITCHELL: Brothers and Sisters can we please observe a minute of silence for our fallen hero *(pause)* thank you. I will now deliver the eulogy. It is with deep regret that we are gathered here today in sympathy with the bereaved family of our late dear Brother William Dickenson, killed in action in Vietnam. Brother Dickenson was a warrior in arms. The hearts of family, friends and relatives, go out to our Brother William's lovely wife, Sister Zera Dickenson.

For many of us this is a very sad occasion. Seems like the only time we get together, family or otherwise, is at a happy or sad occasion such as marriage or death. Although at this time, we all know we are gathered here to give our total support to Sister Zera.

Brother William and I were very dear friends. I never thought the time would come when I would be asked by the family to render his Home-Going service.

My heart was saddened when I received word of Brother William's death. I said "Lord, why?" Why did it have to be Brother William? Being a Reverend and the Senior Pastor of the Faith Tabernacle Baptist Church, I asked the Lord to reach deep down into my heart and soul. I asked him to lift me up and give me strength from my frail weakness to help me through this service.

So I'm here today with your prayers and my trust in God. I know everything will be alright. Can I get an Amen, Brothers and Sisters?

Now let's think about all the good things that Brother William Dickenson represented throughout his life. He would not want us to grieve. He would want us to all go on and live our lives to the fullest. I want you to know and remember that William's spirit lives on in all those hearts that he came in contact with. I want you to know that Brother William has fought his last fight and he doesn't have to fight anymore in Man's earthly Army, Air Force, or whatever. He is a warrior in God's Army of Spiritual Angels who has entered into the pearly gates of heaven and eternal life.

We must prepare ourselves for our day is coming. Life on earth in this physical world is but a temporary thing.

So I ask you my Brothers and Sisters, isn't it wonderful how God has prepared a place for Brother William. I want you to remember that just as Brother William was called upon, there will be a time when you'll be called on too, and rewarded in heavenly glory.

Now I'd like to ask all of you to please stand as the flag is presented to Sister Zera. *(Reverend Mitchell a former Air Force Chaplin presents the American Flag to Sister Zera)*

As the officiating clergy and on behalf of the family, I want to thank all of you for your presence here today. This concludes the Home-Going service of Brother William Dickenson. The family requests your presence at the burial which will be at the Frederick Douglass Cemetery, on Staten Island.

FADE OUT

SCENE IX

THE DAY AFTER THE FUNERAL, MARGARITE CALLS ZERA
ON THE PHONE.

ZERA: *(answers telephone)* Hello

MARGARITE: Hello Zera, it's me, Margarite. *(pause)* I'm calling to
see how you are feeling today?

ZERA: I'm afraid, Margarite. My baby doesn't feel the same inside me
as it did before. It feels like something is wrong. I have stomach
cramps and I'm bleeding. It's like the baby wants to come out.

MARGARITE: Girl, I don't know what's wrong but you sound
terrible. Why didn't you call me? Hang up, I'll call
our doctor. *(pause)* I have the number. Don't worry
Zera, you'll be alright. I'll call you right back. Bye.

FADE OUT

SCENE X

MARGARITE INFORMS ZERA OF HER DOCTOR'S APPOINTMENT.

ZERA: *(answering telephone)* Hello, hello, Margarite is it you?

MARGARITE: Yes, Zera, it's me. The doctor said to bring you in right away, so he can run you through some tests.

ZERA: Margarite I'm scared. Please help me. Come quickly, I hope I'm not having a miscarriage. I hope my baby's okay.

MARGARITE: I'm on my way. Come down when I ring the bell and be careful.

ZERA: Margarite, why me? Why is everything happening to me? Please hurry *(pause)* Thanks.

FADE OUT

<u>SCENE XI</u>

THE FOLLOWING WEEK IN ZERA'S APARTMENT.

ZERA: Why didn't the doctor tell me himself, that the miscarriage was
due to the fetus being stillborn?

MARGARITE: He knew you were already upset and couldn't take
much more. He wanted to wait before explaining
everything. That's why he told you not to give up
hope, because you can still bear children.

ZERA: Oh girl, I can't take any more pain and suffering. I'm torn up
inside. My William is gone and now my baby! Please, Oh God!
Oh God! Help me, please! *(Sobbing profoundly)*

FADE OUT

<u>SCENE XII</u>

DIMLY LIT UNDERGROUND CAVE IN VIETNAM'S INDIAN COUNTRY USED MAINLY FOR INTERROGATING CAPTURED AMERICAN PRISONERS, VC/INTERROGATOR IS WAITING FOR PRISONER TO BE BROUGHT IN BY TWO (VC) VIET CONG SOLDIERS.

VC/INTERROGATOR: Bring in the prisoner. *(a young man is pushed and shoved into the interrogation room by the soldiers. The man is a Marine. He looks like he has seen his last days of war. He is blindfolded, his clothes are tattered, and his hands are tied behind his back.)*

VC/SOLDIER #1: Sit down in this chair you fool, and enjoy a lesson you weren't prepared for when caught by your enemy. Now you are our prisoner. Do you know why you are here?

MARINE: *(as he is directed and pushed to sit down in the chair)* Actually I don't.

VC/INTERROGATOR: You're here because you got caught behind our lines trying to map out our position.

MARINE: *(uncomfortably squirming in his seat)* You bastards, untie me.

VC/SOLDIER #1: *(grabs Marine's head yanking it back)* Shut up your mouth and listen, before I shut it for you.

VC/INTERROGATOR: You're in a pretty bad position to speak out of disrespect. You're so young. Why do you fight in such a ruthless war? You should know by now that you can never win.

MARINE: How do you know?

VC/INTERROGATOR: You are in a bad position to even think about winning. While you are our prisoner, your comrades are out there fighting and dying for freedom in our country.

MARINE: Untie me, take off this blindfold.

VC/SOLDIER #1: You had your chance. You are our enemy and now my prisoner. Tell me the real reason why you are here?

MARINE: I'm here because I'm fighting for my country and I'm helping the South fight Communist aggression.

VC/INTERROGATOR: *(takes out a cigarette as if to smoke it)* Remove the Marine's blindfold.

MARINE: *(as blindfold is removed by VC/Soldier #1)* Thank you!

VC/INTERROGATOR: *(speaking to Marine)* Look around you, does this look like an American installation? You are fighting in the wrong war. Your fight should be back in America, fighting against crime and racism and many other injustices in your own country. Since you are here as our prisoner, you can die here like so many of your American comrades. *(VC/Interrogator points to map on the wall)* Do you see this map? This is Vietnam's Indian country, North, South, East and West.

MARINE: Big deal. *(Struggling to rise from chair, spits on floor)*

VC/SOLDIER #1: *(grabs Marine yanking him back into the chair)* I told you to shut up! And sit down!

VC/INTERROGATOR: Easy, on him, we don't want to make him worse off than he is already. *(walks over and pats Marine on shoulder)* We must leave him some energy to feel the torture of the hill.

MARINE: What hill?

VC/INTERROGATOR: The hill of red ants that will torture you 'til you die, you young American bastard. Have you anything more to say? *(VC/Interrogator lights a cigarette)*

MARINE: I don't have to say anything except my name, rank, service number and date of birth, nothing else. *(VC/Soldier #1, grabs Marine and yanks him up out of the chair)*

VC/INTERROGATOR: *(becomes angry, he takes cigarette from his lips and throws it to the ground crushing it with his foot)* Get him out of here, feed him to the ants. Bring in the next prisoner for interrogation. *(VC/Soldier #1, removes Marine prisoner from interrogation room. VC/Interrogator pours and sips on his cup of coffee. Prisoner wearing tattered Air Force uniform with hands tied behind his back is pushed into the interrogation room by two VC/Soldiers, prisoner stumbles and falls)* Captain Dickenson!

VC/SOLDIER #2: Dickenson! Get up on your feet.

CAPTAIN DICKENSON: I'm moving, you don't have to keep pushing me.

VC/SOLDIER #1: You're not moving fast enough. I said get up, get up on your feet, move. You Americans have been trained well, but you have not been trained for the ultimate.

CAPTAIN DICKENSON: Ultimate, big deal, what's that?

VC/SOLDIER #1: You really want to know? Really! I'll tell you. You are going to go so far that you will wish you never came in touch with me.

CAPTAIN DICKENSON: I demand respect.

VC/SOLDIER #2: *(grabs Captain Dickenson by shirt collar pulling him from the floor to his feet and pushing him to sit down in a chair)* You want respect? I'll give you respect, the same respect you give my people when you rampage through our hamlets, villages, and rice paddies killing and taking prisoners.

CAPTAIN DICKENSON: *(recognizing him)* You're a Viet Cong, you . . . you're the enemy?

VC/SOLDIER #2: Didn't you know? You dumb Americans allow Vietnamese nationals to work on your American installations and bases, and from this we receive some of our most valued information.

CAPTAIN DICKENSON: How could you? You who have cut my hair so many times and given me shaves as my own personal barber and house boy? I thought we were friends!

VC/SOLDIER #2: Friends, really, what would make you think that! When you have lived as I have lived and as the people of this country have lived in time of war, you have but two choices, to live by fighting or die by not fighting. After seeing my father and mother killed, and my wife raped and tortured by the North Vietnamese Army (NVA) I had no choice. I was a young man forced into joining the Viet Cong. My wife begged and pleaded with me not to join with them. I promised her that things would be better for us if I did.

CAPTAIN DICKENSON: You're a traitor, a traitor to your own people of the South and to those who were sent here to help you.

VC/SOLDIER #1: Call me what you want, but I have learned much from the Americans. My wife is one of us. She is working on one of your American bases during the day as a laundry maid, *(laughing)* and providing us with vital information at night.

VC/INTERROGATOR: *(is standing over Captain Dickenson with a clipboard)* Captain Dickenson, would you like a cup of coffee?

CAPTAIN DICKENSON: *(becomes furious)* You filthy gooks.

VC/INTERROGATOR: Captain you should have more respect. A pilot in the Air Force, tell me, what's your name again? Let me see! *(checks clipboard looking for name)* Oh, I see, you are Captain William . . . .

CAPTAIN DICKENSON: That's right, William Dickenson, Captain U.S. Air Force, service number 1222577, date of birth 06/12/47.

VC/INTERROGATOR: Very good, I see you were able to retain something from your military training, *(with his hand, VC/Interrogator, grabs Captain Dickenson's face and squeezes it)* . . . I am the ultimate, the one who determines whether you live or die, and you will respect me as long as you are my prisoner. *(releases hand from Captain Dickenson's face and takes a seat behind desk)* You as an American, my comrades and I have a lot of respect, and especially for trying to fight a war you cannot win.

CAPTAIN DICKENSON: You are to treat all prisoners according to the Geneva Convention.

VC/INTERROGATOR: This is Vietnam, Captain, just as you do not recognize the Napalm and Ordinance you drop on our people, we do not recognize the Geneva Convention. The trouble with you Americans is that you value life and material things too much. You know what, how about you and I making a deal?

CAPTAIN DICKENSON: I don't make any deals with the enemy.

VC/INTERROGATOR: Enemy, you call "us" enemy?

CAPTAIN DICKENSON: That's right.

VC/INTERROGATOR: You're right, Captain Dickenson, we're your enemy and you are our enemy. Who is right, is God on your side?

CAPTAIN DICKENSON: Yes, He is.

VC/INTERROGATOR: How do you know?

CAPTAIN DICKENSON: I just know.

VC/INTERROGATOR: Then you don't know very much, Captain. You are forgetting . . . .

CAPTAIN DICKENSON: I'm not forgetting anything.

VC/INTERROGATOR: Buddha is our wheel of life, and it is through Him we will be Reincarnated to return to continue our mission.

CAPTAIN DICKENSON: Your beliefs are pathetic.

VC/SOLDIER #1: But, we are not afraid to die.

CAPTAIN DICKENSON: Neither am I, I do not fear dying.

VC/SOLDIER #2: You speak very brave, maybe you want to die, the same way the young Marine that just left is to die.

VC/INTERROGATOR: That's too good for him, his death should not come by ants but from a tortured mind. Captain, would you like some coffee or one of your American brand cigarettes?

CAPTAIN DICKENSON: You can't buy me with kindness or favors.

VC/INTERROGATOR: Is that so, I have something of your's that you value very much *(he shows the Captain a wallet)*. Do you see this? To you Americans a picture is worth a thousand words *(he opens the wallet)*. What a beautiful woman!

CAPTAIN DICKENSON: *(angry)* That's my wife's picture.

VC/INTERROGATOR: It's mine now, *(holding up picture in teasing manner and laughing)* it was your's.

CAPTAIN DICKENSON: *(stands up)* Give it here. Why don't you bastard's kill me? Take my life.

VC/SOLDIER #2: You fool, you talk about dying? That's too easy. You must suffer. *(VC/Soldier #2, forces Captain Dickenson back into the chair)*

CAPTAIN DICKENSON: Give me my picture and wallet. She's my wife. She's having my child.

VC/INTERROGATOR: Do you want to see her again? If you do, cooperate with us and give us some strategic

military information. What was the purpose
of your mission?

CAPTAIN DICKENSON: Never, never, I'll die first. I'll tell you
nothing.

VC/INTERROGATOR: Then you don't love your wife. You
wouldn't do her good anyway, because
by now she has probably received word
of you're missing or killed in action.
Captain Dickenson, how does it feel to be
considered dead when you aren't? You are a
prisoner of war, our prisoner.

VC/SOLDIER #2: Cooperate you fool. Maybe we will go easy on
you. Wouldn't you like that? *(Captain Dickenson
ignoring question)*

VC/INTERROGATOR: You are a stubborn man. You will not
cooperate, hmmm? Then, you can forget
about ever seeing your family and friends
again.

CAPTAIN DICKENSON: No! No! No! Why are you doing this to
me?

VC/INTERROGATOR: As far as you're concerned, all of your family
and friends are dead.

CAPTAIN DICKENSON: I don't believe you, I won't believe you! It's
all a lie! I'll never believe you!

VC/INTERROGATOR: *(holding up picture, tearing it, throws pieces to
the floor, stepping on them)* You will believe

me now. She was your wife who was carrying your child. They are dead now. So, as the thought remains in your mind, you are also dead.

CAPTAIN DICKENSON: *(hysterical)* I'll kill you, I'll kill you, or why don't you just kill me! Let me die, you bastards.

VC/INTERROGATOR: *(lights a cigarette and laughs)* It's too late, Captain. Your mind is already dead. I want this prisoner taken North to Hanoi, treat him with kindness.

VC/SOLDIER #1: *(yanking Captain Dickenson from the chair)* Get up you bastard, hold still. This is how we treat American prisoners. Move, I'm no longer your barber, you bastard. I am your enemy and you are my prisoner. *(VC/Interrogator and VC/Soldier #1, laughing)*

———

FADE OUT

<u>SCENE XIII</u>

THE DINNER PARTY

ZERA'S GIRLFRIEND MARGARITE HAS A DINNER PARTY AND INTRODUCES STEVE ROGERS TO ZERA. HE IS EXCITED ABOUT MEETING HER BUT SHE IS VERY SHY. STEVE IS FROM HAMPTON, VIRGINIA, AND LIKES THE NEW YORK SCENE. THEY DEVELOP A SERIOUS RELATIONSHIP. HE PROPOSES TO HER AND THEY ARE MARRIED. THE REALITY OF THE PAST DISRUPTS THEIR MARITAL RELATIONSHIP.

MARGARITE: I want everyone to party, enjoy yourselves and have a good time because I don't have parties often. *(Margarite interrupts Zera)* Excuse me, Zera, can I see you for a minute? There is a real nice gentleman I want you to meet.

ZERA: *(gesturing with open hands)* I know everybody here.

MARGARITE: This man you don't know, Zera.

ZERA: But how do you know I don't know him?

MARGARITE: Because he's from Hampton, Virginia, I met him when he was here visiting New York on business.

ZERA: I don't know, Margarite. I'm really not ready for another serious relationship and I'm certainly not thinking about marriage, not after what I went through.

MARGARITE: Girl! Who said you have to get married? *(doorbell rings)* That must be him, Steve's his name, he said he'd be here around nine o'clock. Excuse me Zera while I get the door. *(as the doorbell rings again she approaches the door)* Just a minute please. *(opening the door she sees Steve)* Oh Steve, I was hoping it was you.

STEVE: Margarite! I'm glad to see you. On the train ride from Virginia, the closer I got to New York, the more excited I became about meeting the young lady you told me about? I can't wait to meet her.

MARGARITE: Alright, Steve, follow me. She's over here. Zera, this is Steve Rogers, the gentleman I spoke about. Steve, this is Zera Dickenson, my best friend. So now I am going to leave you two together so you can get acquainted.

STEVE: Hello, Miss Zera. It's really a pleasure meeting you. The thought of you has been on my mind for quite some time.

ZERA: Thank you, Steve. I don't know what to say, just that I'm, I'm . . .

STEVE: What, a bit shy?

ZERA: I am, I guess, sort of.

STEVE: Well, Zera, you don't have to be shy with me. You can talk about anything you want.

ZERA: I was surprised by my best friend Margarite. She said she was having a dinner party and had invited someone she wanted me to meet. She just mentioned your name a few minutes ago. Actually, I'm really impressed to meet someone new.

STEVE: Well, I hope I didn't shock you too much. You know something? With all this good music playing, why are we letting it go to waste? Would you like to dance?

ZERA: Sure, I'd love to, are you a good dancer?

———

FADE OUT

<u>SCENE XIV</u>

ZERA IS SITTING ON A PARK BENCH OVERLOOKING A LAKE. SHE IS READING A NEWSPAPER AND WAITING FOR MARGARITE.

MARGARITE: *(approaching the bench carrying a brown bag)* Hey, girl, what's happening?

ZERA: I'm just here enjoying the calmness of the breeze.

MARGARITE: *(sits on bench next to Zera)* I'm sorry if I'm a little late but you know how those darn buses are.

ZERA: Oh, that's alright. I thought I was late myself.

MARGARITE: How long have you been waiting?

ZERA: *(looking at her watch)* Oh, only about fifteen, twenty minutes.

MARGARITE: I know I would have been here about forty-five minutes ago but the darn bus broke down. Out of all the five boroughs, Staten Island has the worst public transportation. I don't know what's worse, breaking down in the summer or not showing up in the winter. I just don't know. *(pause)* This island was really beautiful when we were growing up, but look how it has changed.

ZERA: Yes, it's really a shame the way certain sections have deteriorated, it's really depressing. I blame the people.

MARGARITE: I blame the people and the politicians. Look at Stapleton, Port Richmond, everything is damn near torn down. What we have here is a new brand of people, they don't give a damn about themselves or anything else.

ZERA: *(looking at Margarite's bag)* What's in the bag?

MARGARITE: Oh I'm sorry, I have two sandwiches . . . *(gives sandwich to Zera)* Here, this is lunch.

ZERA: Thanks, girl. You're a real friend.

MARGARITE: That's alright, we've known each other since the fifth grade and our friendship is still the same.

ZERA: *(they begin eating the sandwiches)* I can remember 'til this day, when you moved to 110 Henry Street from 131 Corson Avenue.

MARGARITE: My sisters and brothers didn't like the move either but we had no choice. My mother was moving away from my stepfather because he started to treat her badly after the birth of my baby brother. *(Margarite starts crying)* We could not take my baby brother Ricky with us. My stepfather said Ricky was his child and if my mother wanted to leave, she could take us and go, but not Ricky. He didn't care; we were only his stepchildren.

ZERA: Come on, calm down. You know I'm your friend and we'll always be friends. You know something, girl?

MARGARITE: What Zera?

ZERA: You made my outlook seem brighter.

MARGARITE: I did. How?

ZERA: You remember the state of mind I was in after the news of William's death?

MARGARITE: I remember clearly, you looked like you just wanted to lay down and die.

ZERA: It was such a heavy burden to live with. I just couldn't believe that my William's charred remains were before my very eyes sealed up in a flag draped coffin. Oh, how I was hurting. I tried so hard to convince myself that it wasn't true. The pain I felt was unbearable. Thinking of having to live with it for the rest of my life was the thing causing me to want to give up.

MARGARITE: I'll never forget William. He was so well liked. His funeral will always remain in my mind because I had never experienced a funeral service so sad. Zera, everybody there hurt and felt the pain with you. When you think back so many of the young men with whom we grew up, dated, hung out, partied, and went to school with are no longer here. They died in Vietnam or died on the streets from drugs and over dosing after they came home from the war.

ZERA: We had some good times, didn't we?

MARGARITE: We sure did, girl, especially the weekends, they were the joint.

ZERA: That's right, it was you, me, Mildred, Barbara, all of us. We'd all wind up at the Paramount or the St. George Theatres. We would watch the double, sometimes triple feature movies and cartoons, while in-between kissing and hugging our boyfriends.

MARGARITE: Speaking of hugging and kissing, Mildred never forgave Barbara for sleeping with her man. What was his name, again? *(pause)* Ray, that's right.

ZERA: But Barbara was on the wild side with all that drinking and smoking.

MARGARITE: Let's not forget Hot in the Pants! And you know how she used to wear her clothes . . . . hardly on.

ZERA: You know I've been trying to get those girls to speak for years. I love them both but I wonder if they'll ever let bygones be bygones. We all grew up with arguments and differences but we still were close. I've always tried to be the peacemaker, those were the days. William and I had started getting serious. We were very much in love but whenever it came to the action war movies, William's eyes were glued to the screen. There wasn't a chance of getting a kiss because he kept his mouth full of popcorn. He would sit on the edge of his seat cheering for the good guys. You know, I actually thought he was feeling the war experience coming directly from the giant screen. It was like he was totally involved in the action, especially when the Marines were hitting the beach against the Japanese in the movie Guadalcanal Diary.

MARGARITE: William really had it in his blood, didn't he?

ZERA: Yes he did, and he once told me, if he joined any branch of service it would be the Marines.

MARGARITE: How did he get into the Air Force?

ZERA: His mother and I talked him into it. We said to him, why not the Air Force? He just looked at us and smiled. So, the Air

Force is where he died. We thought it would be safer. We had no idea he would be a fighter pilot.

MARGARITE: There's one thing Zera, about any military service, in time of war none are safe.

ZERA: You know something?

MARGARITE: What?

ZERA: Ever since you gave that dinner party and introduced me to Steve, I feel like the young school girl I was when William and I were dating.

MARGARITE: Girl, that's a sign.

ZERA: A sign, what kind of a sign, Margarite?

MARGARITE: You're in love with Steve. What else could it be?

ZERA: I don't know, but he said that he feels the same way I do, but only it's deeper.

MARGARITE: Don't tell me, girl, did he propose to you?

Zera: *(pause)* Yes, he did.

MARGARITE: Wow! If I ever heard of good news, this has got to be the biggest event that has hit Staten Island in a very long time. You know something girl? I don't know why it is that my girlfriends have all the luck when it comes to finding a decent man. I'm happy for you.

ZERA: If it weren't for you inviting me to the dinner party and introducing me to Steve, none of this would be happening. I'd still be down and out in my depressed state, thinking about how my happiness with William had been snuffed out.

MARGARITE: Think nothing about it girl. I want you to be happy and since you and Steve have hit it off well, go for it. What do you have to lose? The Lord has found another way to make you happy by bringing someone special into your life. I want you to be happy because if anyone deserves happiness, it has to be you girl.

ZERA: But what about you?

MARGARITE: Don't worry about me. If things don't go right for me and Mr. Right doesn't come into my life soon, I'll just take it in stride. I'll live my life to the fullest and be like an old maid.

ZERA: Are you serious?

MARGARITE: Sure, girl, I'm as serious as we are here sitting in the park talking about it. *(looking at the time on her watch)* Hey girl, it's getting late. I think we have talked enough.

ZERA: *(stands up)* You know, I really enjoyed our talk today and I'm glad you're my best friend.

MARGARITE: And I'm glad your mine, now when is the big day?

ZERA: I really didn't give him a definite date.

MARGARITE: Zera, why not?

ZERA: Actually, the thought of William sometimes comes and goes in my mind when I'm with Steve. Knowing they were both in the Air Force stationed at the same base in Vietnam makes me feel guilty. It's almost like William is watching our every move.

MARGARITE: Girl you got to erase that thought from your mind, and think of it as William wanting you to be happy. By the way, did Steve know William?

ZERA: He mentioned him on occasion. I think they were in the same squadron.

MARGARITE: Come on girl, cheer up. Think of it as William wanting it to be this way.

ZERA: It does make a lot of sense. *(smiling)* I think I'll give him that definite date when I see him later tonight.

MARGARITE: Go ahead girl. *(they leave, walking away smiling)*

—————

FADE OUT

SCENE XV

ZERA AND STEVE, NOW MARRIED, LATE AT NIGHT IN THEIR APARTMENT, ONE YEAR AFTER THE DINNER PARTY.

STEVE: *(enters apartment and turns on the light and walks over to the sofa where Zera is asleep)* Honey, I'm home, *(he gives her a kiss and sits down next to her)* Honey, I said I'm home.

ZERA: I know, I heard you come in. You are home late again tonight.

STEVE: You know my responsibilities and that I don't get any help.

ZERA: No, I don't know!

STEVE: There is always something new coming up and I have to stay late because of my position as Vice-President.

ZERA: Steve, how much longer will these late nights keep us apart?

STEVE: Not much longer, Bob will be retiring soon and I will get the job of President. Then I'll be calling the shots and therefore, no more long hours and late nights coming home. I really love you Sweetheart.

ZERA: *(smiling and stroking Steve's head)* I love you too, Honey! Can we go to bed?

STEVE: *(they both get up from the sofa)* You know something, Sweetheart, that's the best thing I've heard all day.

ZERA: *(walking with Steve to the bedroom)* Do you need me to set the clock to wake you?

STEVE: I'll be alright!

ZERA: *(she sets the clock and turns off the light)* Goodnight Steve.

STEVE: *(kissing Zera)* I love you Honey. Goodnight.

FADE OUT

<h1 style="text-align:center">SCENE XVI</h1>

MORNING BREAKFAST, SHE ENTERS BEDROOM TO AWAKE STEVE.

ZERA: *(A.M., clock alarms)* Steve, wake up, . . . it's time to get up.

STEVE: Is it six already?

ZERA: Yes! Now get up!

STEVE: It seems as though I just went to bed.

ZERA: You did! Now get up!

STEVE: What's for breakfast?

ZERA: What do you want?

STEVE: I'll settle for the usual dish of scrambled eggs and cheese, potatoes, toast, and juice. The works!

ZERA: (returning to kitchen) Breakfast is ready!

STEVE: I'll be right there!

ZERA: *(sitting down at table)* Come eat before the food gets cold. *(Steve enters kitchen surprised and sits at table)* I already knew what you wanted for breakfast, so I had it almost finished before I called you to get up. Steve, there's something I want to tell you. I don't know if this is the right time to approach you with it because I know how dedicated you are to your job.

STEVE: This meal, is outta sight! *(pause)* Oh, oh, excuse me, what did you say?

ZERA: Oh, forget it.

STEVE: *(he looks at his watch)* I'm sorry but can we talk about it when I get home this evening. I have to finish getting dressed.

ZERA: Okay, will you be home late again tonight?

STEVE: I'll phone you.

ZERA: Yes, please, so I'll know whether or not to put away the food.

STEVE: *(kisses Zera before he leaves)* This is our busy season and I have to get the reports to send out for the corporation by next week's deadline.

ZERA: Have a good day. I love you.

STEVE: *(leaving apartment)* Thank you. I love you too. Talk to you later.

ZERA: *(begins her household chores, phone rings, she answers it)* Hello, Rogers residence. *(pause)* I'm sorry Sir, but you must have the wrong number. The Dickensons do not live here. *(pause)* You said you're trying to locate a Zera Dickenson, may I ask with whom am I speaking? *(pause)* I'm asking because your voice seems so familiar, almost as if you were my late husband. Now, what did you say, William Dickenson? I'm sorry Sir, but you cannot be my late husband. There is nothing for you to explain. I don't have time for your nonsense. I know my husband is dead I have proof. *(she slams down the phone)*

FADE OUT

SCENE XVII

ZERA'S SURPRISE VISITOR

ZERA: *(doorbell rings)* Who is it?

WILLIAM: It's me, William!

ZERA: William who?

WILLIAM: William Dickenson!

ZERA: William Dickenson, what do you want?

WILLIAM: What do I want? I've got something important to speak with you about. Come on, Zera, let me come in.

ZERA: Come back when my husband is at home.

WILLIAM: What husband? I'm your husband. I need to speak with you now. It's very important. Open the door. *(Zera opens the door)* Hello, Zera, what's wrong? Don't you remember me? Don't you remember the good times we shared together, before I left for the Air Force and was sent to Vietnam back in late 1965?

ZERA: *(shocked)* My William is dead!

WILLIAM: You were expecting our baby. I heard you married some Air Force dude that was stationed in Vietnam at the Da Nang Air Base. Come to think of it the name Rogers, Steve Rogers rings a bell.

ZERA: Yes, he was at the base but, my William is dead!

WILLIAM: *(with anxiety, he grabs and embraces her)* Look at me, look at my eyes, does my touch feel like that of a dead man to you? The real reason I came here today is to see our little boy, or is it a little girl? *(he breaks embrace trying to look beyond her into the apartment)* I just know he or she should be pretty big by now.

ZERA: But, William, you're dead. You were killed in action according to the military reports. We had the funeral, the flagged draped coffin, and the Purple Heart that I received from the military.

William: *(annoyed)* Well, Zera, I'm not dead. I'm as much alive as you are. I was captured, a POW Prisoner of War. Now where is my child?

ZERA: *(sadly)* There is no child, William.

WILLIAM: What? . . . What do you mean no child? Let's not play games, Zera. I've searched all over to find you and now you tell me there is no child, no son or daughter!

ZERA: William, there is no child because the shock of your death caused me to have a miscarriage.

WILLIAM: Please, Lord, not me. Oh, please, no! No! No! Let it not be true. I can't believe I was cursed by the enemy, fighting for my country. *(irrational, turning away to act out frustrations)* You damn enemy interrogators! Look what you've done to me. You ruined my happiness and my life just as you said you would. *(embraces Zera)* I still love you and want you back regardless, whether or not you're able to face a hard decision. This is my other reason for wanting to see you. I wanted to talk to you today but I guess I can't. I'll just leave but I'll be back when your husband is home. It wouldn't be right to talk about him to you when he's not here. I want to meet him and I do want him to know how I feel about you, even if it means that one of us will be hurt.

ZERA: *(pushing his arms away from her)* What do you mean?

WILLIAM: Do you still have strong feelings for me, Zera? Don't you still care? Don't you still love me?

ZERA: William, I really can't say at this point because it's like I'm reliving a nightmare or maybe more like a television soap opera or something. I really need to talk this thing over, especially with my husband Steve. Right now, Steve and I are married and have each other, and I feel quite happy.

WILLIAM: Okay, think it over, but I'll be back. *(exiting doorway he looks back)* So long, Zera, I'll see you and Steve later. Zera, I'm not dead. As you can see, I'm very much alive.

ZERA: *(standing in the doorway watching William leave)* This is unreal. *(closes the door and shakes her head)* William, William. I know my William is dead.

FADE OUT

SCENE XVIII

STEVE ARRIVES HOME FROM WORK.

STEVE: *(opens door and enters apartment)* Honey, I'm home.

ZERA: You're home early today.

STEVE: *(putting his jacket and briefcase down, he kisses Zera)* Not much happened at work today. How was your day?

ZERA: You wouldn't believe it but my day seemed so much like a television soap opera.

STEVE: You mean to say it seemed that real?

ZERA: I'm not joking, Steve. Believe me, what happened today was a very traumatic experience. After you left for work this morning the phone rang. I answered it because I thought it was you but I was wrong. The person with whom I spoke, his voice seemed strange but familiar. I thought this person had a wrong number.

STEVE: *(listening, he sits down on the couch to read his newspaper)* Zera, what is it you are trying to tell me?

ZERA: *(she sits down at table)* This person I spoke with claimed to be my late husband, William.

STEVE: Zera, Zera, according to the report William is dead. His aircraft was hit with antiaircraft fire, it burst into flames and went down over Haiphong. Then what about when we first met and you told me about him, the funeral services, and his sealed coffin with charred remains. If the man who called you is William, then who or what is buried in the cemetery?

ZERA: Well, Steve, believe it or not, I talked with someone on the phone that sounded like him. I told him my William is dead. He insisted and said he had something personal he wanted to speak to me about.

STEVE: Zera, I think what you're telling me is a soap opera or maybe a bad dream.

ZERA: *(doorbell rings)* It is not a soap opera, he was here. I'll tell you the rest after I answer the door. *(she proceeds to the door and upon opening it, she sees William)*

STEVE: Zera, who is it? If that's the paperboy tell him I'll pay him next week. *(Zera not answering, Steve goes to the door. He is shocked at the sight of William standing in the doorway)*

WILLIAM: Steve, Zera, you both look as though you are shocked at seeing me. Zera, I can understand Steve staring but for you, it should not be a surprise. Remember I was here earlier today. *(Zera leaves walking toward the kitchen)*

STEVE: *(turns his back to get his thoughts together, then faces William)* William, you were killed, shot down on a reconnaissance mission near Haiphong in '66! First, you were listed as "missing in action" then according to the reports, it was changed to killed in action. Charred remains were found by the wreckage of your aircraft. *(Steve walks toward table to get himself a drink. William closes the door and walks into the living room)*

WILLIAM: Well, Steve, do I look dead to you? Or perhaps you are hallucinating that you are seeing and talking to a ghost. I received the same stare from Zera. Well, here I am, very much alive. Steve, I guess you know why I am here?

STEVE: *(sips his drink then turns to face William and speaks sternly)* No, I don't.

WILLIAM: Then, I guess Zera didn't tell you. I called earlier trying to locate her. I wanted to come over to speak with her personally.

STEVE: *(annoyed)* Why and about what?

WILLIAM: I wanted to talk about us, her and about me!

STEVE: *(walking toward William and looking directly in his face)* What do you mean about her and about you?

WILLIAM: *(throws up his hands)* Look man, back off. I know you probably don't want to hear it, but I'm going to say it anyway. Zera was my wife before she became your's. I still love that woman, and I need her so we can continue our life where we left off . . . .

STEVE: *(interrupts)* Wait a minute, what do you mean, where you left off? What you need to do is get the hell out of here, leave.

WILLIAM: We were both happy together and she was expecting our child. That all changed due to wrong reports of my being killed and it was the main cause of her miscarriage. After that ordeal, her dream of having our child was never fulfilled. She spent a long time suffering the loss. Being lonely probably gave her reason to find herself another man who would try to fulfill her dreams.

STEVE: *(annoyed)* Let me tell you something, I'm fulfilling her dreams so forget what you had together.

WILLIAM: It's not that easy, Steve. Zera and I spoke earlier this morning.

STEVE: *(agitated)* I don't care when you spoke, but . . . you can forget about Zera. The love you and she had before is over. I'm not going to allow you to spoil our happiness by coming here trying to make a change after she had suffered all those years of loneliness. We are both happy together and we love each other. *(violently pulling William and shoving him to the door)* Good-bye, William. Get out of here.

WILLIAM: *(forcefully pushing Steve back)* Steve, be reasonable! Let's talk like we have some sense.

STEVE: *(angered)* I am about as reasonable as I'm going to be. Besides, our acquaintance in Vietnam was a short one. I met Zera at a friends dinner party. If it weren't for that, I probably wouldn't know her or be with her now. She never talked very much about you. She seemed to be in a state of depression and loneliness. After several times seeing her and us getting to know each other, we decided to get hitched. I didn't tell her I knew you. I didn't want her to continue suffering from her two losses, you being killed and the miscarriage.

WILLIAM: Steve, what do you know about suffering unless you have experienced it? Do you know what it's like to be a prisoner of war?

STEVE: Yeah! Quite frankly I do!

WILLIAM: Well, so do I. I know what it feels like to be considered dead when you aren't. I know what it feels like to have your mind tormented and messed over by the enemy, and to hear your own name and Hanoi Hattie reading casualty reports over Radio Hanoi. Do you know what it's like to have your family's pictures ripped from your wallet? Do you know what it's like to be tormented and mentally abused with words and told your family is dead and you'll never see them again? Do you Steve? *(grabbing Steve's shirt)* Huh? Do you know what it's like?

STEVE: *(pushing William's hands off his shirt)* Look man, get your hands off me. I don't know what it is like, only what I went through as a POW. I've seen many a man die from that kind of trauma.

WILLIAM: It was a hell that I lived through during years of constant abuse and insane animalistic conditions. I suffered this and much more, all because I did not cooperate with and give the enemy information. I was kept alive for their own pleasure of destroying my mental being. I finally made my escape with two others from that hellish nightmare.

STEVE: Okay William! You stated your reason for this visit and what you've experienced as a captured POW I truly sympathize with you, I was there. Now are you finished? It's time for you to say good-bye. *(Steve pushes William toward the door and William, protecting himself, pushes Steve away)*

WILLIAM: Hey! You think it's going to be that easy. I'm not going to leave just like that, no way Steve, no way! Does Zera know about your misadventures overseas? Did you tell her, Steve? Huh? Did you?

ZERA: *(entering living room with a tray and puts it on the table)* What was that I heard? Steve, is there something I should know that you have not told me?

STEVE: *(pointing his finger at William)* You're asking for trouble man, you better leave while the going is good.

WILLIAM: Well, Steve are you going to tell her or should I? You'll make it easier for yourself if you do.

ZERA: *(looking at Steve)* I'm waiting, tell me.

STEVE: *(agitated)* Okay! William, go ahead and tell her if you think it will make you feel better, *(raising his voice)* but I'm warning you.

WILLIAM: *(turning to Zera)* Did Steve tell you about his homosexual activities with a guy he was friendly with overseas? *(William looks at Steve)* I bet you kept that a secret. Huh, Steve?

STEVE: Man! *(Steve grabs William and throws him down to the floor, stands over him with his fist ready to hit him)* I'm going to kick your ass!

ZERA: *(trying to separate the two men)* Steve stop, both of you, stop! *(shocked and angry, Zera looks at Steve and William)* William, get up! *(as William gets up from the floor)* Steve is this true, is it?

STEVE: *(looking at Zera)* Yeah! But I had my reasons, *(speaking to William)* and who are you to talk? I should still whip your ass, man! You know for a fact that there were a lot of strange things going on in Nam. That's why you often hear the phrase that war is hell and, *(speaking to Zera)* I didn't think you'd understand.

ZERA: Understand! Steve, do you think I understand? Why haven't you told me? What makes you think I would feel any different now, than if I were told before? And now to you William, why did you have to confront me with this? And please Steve, please tell me, is there anymore I should know because I can't take much more of this, especially in my condition.

STEVE: Condition! What condition?

ZERA: I have tried to tell you but you can never find the time to listen. It's always later when you get home, but when you get home it's too late to talk. It seems as though you are more concerned with reaching your goal as President of the Happy Holiday Resort Corporation or has it been your gay activity? If you had not been confronted by William, I still would not have known anything. Isn't that true?

STEVE: William, to you and others it might seem wrong, but I have succeeded in getting what I want in life.

ZERA: You speak of life! What about my life? What about the life of our child, Steve? My husband, a homosexual, and this one comes back from the dead! *(hysterically)* What am I going to do? I'm pregnant, pregnant carrying your child, Steve, our child.

STEVE: *(approaching Zera)* You're pregnant? We're having a baby?

WILLIAM: Zera, that's nice, baby or no baby, I want to know which one of us do you really want, is it him or is it me?

ZERA: *(sternly speaking)* Just like you're asking me about that, what I really want to know is who's thinking about me and the birth of my child? I don't want to go through what I went through before and lose another baby. You guys have got a lot of nerve trying to take control of me. Well, I don't think I can deal with it. I have had one traumatic experience already and I'm not about to become a pawn in a game of chess. This is a new life I'm talking about.

STEVE: What are you trying to say, Zera?

WILLIAM: Yeah! I would like to know, too?

ZERA: You're telling me you want me to make a choice, okay! I'll make it. I don't want either of you. You have no right making me choose between the two of you. Both of you are making me feel sick to my stomach. I don't need this burden on me now, I'd rather be by myself.

STEVE: But, Zera, I love you. I need you. What happened was years ago. Please forgive me for not sharing that with you. I thought it would destroy your love for me and our marriage.

ZERA: *(annoyed with both men)* You assumed that I would not understand. You didn't believe in me enough to confide in me. You didn't even give me the benefit of the doubt. And you, William, do you think you can just come back into my life like that? After years of torment, do you think I would go back to you because you're a war veteran and have pity on you. Well, my former husband, you are sadly mistaken. I'm the one here who's truly been hurt. I want both of you to leave me alone. I need some time to think.

WILLIAM & STEVE: But Zera *(she throws up her hands and walks into the bedroom)*

STEVE: Well, William, I hope you're satisfied. Now get the hell out of my apartment! *(Steve opens the door and pushes William out into the hallway and slams the door closed. Steve walks to the table to get his drink and sits down on sofa, thinking and recapping what has happened. Zera entering room sees Steve. She turns to go back but he notices her)* Zera, please sit down. I need to talk to you *(he takes her hand, they sit together on the couch).*

ZERA: *(crying)* About what? Don't you think I have been hurt enough today?

STEVE: *(wiping tears from Zera's cheeks)* Honey, you've been hurt more than enough and I want things to be different.

ZERA: In what way?

STEVE: By starting our life over again from right now because we are going to be parents, mother and father. Don't you want our child to be the happiest child in the world?

ZERA: I do. I want all of us to be happy.

STEVE: You do? Can you find it in your heart to forgive me, and my past, and to forget about William ever coming back? Huh, baby? Tell me. *(sobbing)*

ZERA: Steve the past is forgotten and that new life is right here in my womb. *(Zera takes Steve's hand and places it on her stomach, they hug and kiss)*

FADE OUT

ACT II

JAHAD'S DREAM

JAHAD'S DAY AT SCHOOL IS SADDENED BY THE TRAGIC NEWS ABOUT THE DEATH OF THE PARENTS OF HIS TWO CLASSMATES. JAHAD ARRIVES HOME FROM SCHOOL AND HIS MOTHER NOTICES THE STRANGE EMOTIONAL LOOK ON HER SON'S FACE. SHE QUESTIONS HIM ABOUT HIS DAY. JAHAD THEN TELLS HIS MOTHER ABOUT HIS DREAM. JAHAD IS THE SON OF STEVE AND ZERA.

SCENE I

ZERA IS AT HOME, IN THE LIVING ROOM, CLEANING. THE DOOR OPENS AND CLOSES. FOOTSTEPS CAN BE HEARD, JAHAD'S ARRIVING HOME FROM SCHOOL.

ZERA: *(looks at Jahad with a serious face)* Jahad, why are you crying? School couldn't have been that bad today. *(holding out her arms gesturing to Jahad)* Come here, where's Mommy's kiss? *(Jahad walks to her but does not hug her)* What's wrong, Jahad? Tell Mommy. *(she grabs his hands, looks at him)*

JAHAD: *(with his head down, mumbles)* I don't know, Mommy.

ZERA: What did you say? I didn't hear you, Jahad.

JAHAD: *(looks at her)* I don't know, Mommy.

ZERA: *(pulls Jahad into her arms)* Now give Mommy a big hug and kiss. Tell me what happened at school today, *(he hugs and kisses her and she wipes the tears away from his face with her finger)* now that's better.

JAHAD: *(seriously looking at his mother)* Mommy, why do daddies and mommies have to die and leave their children to grow up all alone?

ZERA: Jahad, why do you ask such a question?

JAHAD: My teacher cried in school today.

ZERA: What made her cry? Was she not feeling well?

JAHAD: She was crying because Robbin and Cindy weren't in school today *(speaking with his fingers to his mouth)* because, because . . . .

ZERA: Because what, Jahad? Sit here and tell me.

JAHAD: Because their Mommy and Daddy are gone! They died, Mommy. *(he starts to cry)* My teacher said they died in a car accident. My whole class cried.

ZERA: *(she hugs him tightly and kisses him)* Oh no, honey, Mommy can't explain. Did the teacher say how it happened?

JAHAD: The teacher said their car was hit by a big truck that went through a traffic red light. *(pause)* Mommy, I had a dream last night that Daddy is going to die.

ZERA: Jahad, dreams aren't always true.

JAHAD: Please, Mommy, promise me that you and Daddy won't leave
me to grow up by myself like Robbin and Cindy's Mom and
Dad did.

ZERA: I promise. Now you go get started on your homework while
I get started in the kitchen. I know Daddy will be home soon
and he'll be hungry and tired after a hard day's work.

———

FADE OUT

<u>SCENE II</u>

ZERA IS IN THE KITCHEN AND JAHAD IS IN THE LIVING ROOM DOING HIS HOMEWORK. STEVE ARRIVES HOME.

STEVE: Hello, Jahad. *(Steve enters living room with arms extended)*

JAHAD: Daddy, Daddy . . . . *(Jahad runs to hug his dad)*

STEVE: And how is my little man today?

JAHAD: Okay, I guess, Daddy.

STEVE: You guess? Well, you can tell me all about it when you finish your homework. Where's your mother?

JAHAD: Mommy's in the kitchen fixing dinner.

ZERA: *(exits kitchen walking toward Steve, puts her arms around his neck and kisses him on his lips then looks into his eyes)* Mmmmm, hi, Honey!

STEVE: *(they kiss, Steve holding her tight, rubs his hands up and down her back)* Mmmmm, Baby! Let's have a replay of that. *(they kiss)*

ZERA: And how is my lover today after such a hard day at work?

STEVE: Fine, just fine.

ZERA: *(pulls herself from his embrace, he pulls her closer to him)* You'll be even finer after you get out of those clothes, take a hot bath and relax. I'll go run a tub of water for your bath.

STEVE: That won't be necessary Baby, you're doing too much already. You know, I love you and Jahad very much. I'm very thankful for having such a wonderful loving wife and son.

ZERA: I can never do too much Steve. You bring out the love in me with your warm tender care, that's why there is so much love coming from Jahad and me.

STEVE: *(grabbing her waist)* Baby, you don't know how you just made me feel. Come here, Jahad, you belong here too. Come on over and get some of this family love. We both love you, Jahad. You are the life that brought the joy to your mother and me. When your mother carried you in her womb we couldn't wait for you to arrive.

JAHAD: Really, Daddy?

STEVE: Yes, Son.

ZERA: Jahad, if we don't let your father get washed we won't finish eating until late. Now go finish your homework.

JAHAD: Okay Mommy.

ZERA: And as for you, my lover man, you get yourself washed so we can eat and relax.

STEVE: *(rubbing the side of her left thigh and smiling)* Baby! Mmmm, I can't wait.

ZERA: *(smiling)* Wait for what?

STEVE: You know *(playfully grabs her buns)*, bed time!

ZERA: *(blushing, turns and looks at Jahad and back at Steve)* Now Steve, you know this isn't the time and place for such activity, especially in front of . . . .

STEVE: He knows already. I bet he listens at our bedroom door.

JAHAD: Yeah, I do Daddy.

STEVE: See, Zera, he knows. It's hard to keep things a secret with kids these days.

ZERA: I know, especially with a father like you. *(kisses Steve then smiles)*

STEVE: Now, what was that for?

ZERA: For being a good father and a damn good husband. Now, you go and get washed. I'll finish what I have to do in the kitchen, then we can all sit down and enjoy our meal together.

STEVE: *(kisses Zera)* Okay, Baby.

FADE OUT

PROLOGUE

MARGARITE WAS MARRIED TO SOMEONE NAMED ROBERT. SHE THOUGHT HE WAS THE MAN OF HER DREAMS. THE MARRIAGE DIDN'T LAST BECAUSE OF PHYSICAL AND MENTAL ABUSE. THE ONLY POSITIVE OUTCOME WAS THEIR DAUGHTER, LILLIAN. LATER MARGARITE AND WILLIAM DEVELOPED A CLOSE RELATIONSHIP AND EVENTUALLY MARRIED. THIS NOW CREATED A STRONGER BOND BETWEEN ZERA AND MARGARITE. THERE WERE NEVER NEGATIVE FEELINGS ABOUT MARGARITE MARRYING ZERA'S FORMER HUSBAND. IN FACT, BOTH COUPLES BECAME BEST FRIENDS INCLUDING THEIR CHILDREN.

<h1 style="text-align:center"><u>SCENE III</u></h1>

LIVING ROOM, EARLY MORNING HOURS, WILLIAM IS HEARING VOICES AND HALLUCINATING ABOUT HIS CAPTURE. HIS WIFE MARGARITE IS CONCERNED ABOUT HIS SAFETY AND THE AFFECT HIS CONDITION WILL HAVE ON HER DAUGHTER, LILLIAN.

VC/INTERROGATOR: Bring in the next prisoner!

VC/SOLDIER #1: Get up, you, get to your feet.

WILLIAM: *(William stumbles and falls to the floor, moaning, jerking, struggling, trying to get up, yelling and hallucinating)* I'm moving, you don't have to keep pushing me. You're a traitor, a traitor to your own people. I don't make deals with the enemy. That's my wife's picture, give it here. She's having my child. I don't believe you, I won't believe you! It's all a lie! I'll never believe you!

VC/SOLDIER #2: You want respect? I give you respect, same respect you give my people.

WILLIAM: You filthy gooks.

VC/INTERROGATOR: You failed to learn. You do not disrespect your superiors. I am your superior. I am the ultimate, respect me. Are you ready to make a deal?

WILLIAM: I don't make deals with the enemy.

VC/INTERROGATOR: Your wife is dead, your child is dead. Dead, dead, dead!

WILLIAM: *(on the floor, trying to kick at his invisible enemy, he tries to get up)* No! No! No! Kill me! Kill me! . . . I'll die first. Get your hands off me.

MARGARITE: *(hearing noise she runs from the bedroom into the living room, sees William on the floor and becomes afraid. He struggles to stand and runs past her. Margarite grabs him but he pushes her and she falls. She nervously gets up shaking and yelling)* William, William! Lord, why don't you take these hallucinations away from my husband, he's a good man. *(William runs past Margarite as she stumbles and he runs to the sofa. She goes after him and struggles with him on the sofa, yelling)* William, William, wake up! Please wake up, it's only a dream. William, it was a bad dream! You're soaked with sweat.

WILLIAM: *(puts his arms tightly around her)* Did I have another one? Did I hurt you? I can't get rid of these night sweats, headaches, and hallucinations. I'm always on the run. I'm running for my life any which way I can and hearing the enemy's voices. I always see the same faces because Charlie owns the night. He always sneaks up, attempting to slit my throat and leaving me dying in a pool of my own blood.

MARGARITE: No, William, you didn't hurt me this time. I was careful.

WILLIAM: I'm glad you didn't get hurt. I love you Margarite, I love you.

LILLIAN: *(exits from her bedroom)* Mommy, Daddy, what's wrong? What was all the noise, yelling, and screaming?

MARGARITE: Your Daddy had a nightmare.

LILLIAN: *(hugs her father)* Daddy, are you okay?

WILLIAM: Everything is okay, honey, I'm fine. You can go back to bed.

LILLIAN: Okay, thanks Daddy *(kisses parents)* I'm going back to sleep now.

———

FADE OUT

<h1 style="text-align:center">SCENE IV</h1>

FOLLOWING DAY (ZERA'S LIVING ROOM) SHE IS DUSTING AND POLISHING THE FURNITURE WHILE LISTENING TO THE RADIO. THE PHONE RINGS, SHE STOPS TO ANSWER IT.

ZERA: Hello, Rogers residence *(pause)* Margarite why are you crying? *(pause)* Do you want me to come over to comfort you? *(pause)* I was only dusting the furniture. I can come over, it's no problem. *(pause)* Jahad won't be home until four o'clock because his class went to the Staten Island Zoo. *(pause)* Why don't you come over here? *(pause)* We can talk about it. *(pause)* Please Margarite, that's what friends are for. If I were not concerned I wouldn't be asking you to come over. *(pause)* Now stop crying I'll be expecting you in a little while, bye. *(Zera hangs up phone and continuing to clean, looks up at ceiling)* I wonder what could possibly be wrong? *(few minutes pass, then a knock on the door)* Margarite, is that you?

MARGARITE: Yes!

ZERA: *(opens the door)* Margarite, are you still crying? Come in, *(she grabs Margarite by the arm and brings her inside)* Here, have a seat, sit down. Can I get you something to calm your nerves?

MARGARITE: *(wiping her tears with a handkerchief)* I don't know what it is, but William . . .

ZERA: William what?

MARGARITE: William has been acting strange lately.

Zera: Acting strange? How?

MARGARITE: He had another of those prisoner of war nightmares again last night. Only this time he wasn't in bed. He was crouched up beside the sofa and the wall. He was yelling and sounded so pitiful.

ZERA: Oh my God, has he been to the Veterans Hospital lately?

MARGARITE: No, he doesn't go anymore. He doesn't want to have anything to do with the place. He says his mind has been messed over enough by the enemy; the thought of going there for psycho-therapy is like being interrogated all over again. He's tired of getting a bunch of pills and seeing so many homeless veterans walking around like zombies. William is always agitated, frustrated, depressed, and has these mood swings and isolated moments. I make sure I give him his space but I'm afraid his condition is going to affect me and Lillian. She keeps asking me, why is Daddy like that? The only answer I can give is that Daddy was in the Vietnam War and I think it did something to him. I guess things must have been beautiful for you and William before he left for the war.

ZERA: They were beautiful but all the hell I went through, suffering during those years of him being dead but not dead, and of course the miscarriage was awful. His shocking return hit me like a nightmare. Out of depression he came back to break up Steve and me, and to see his child. He didn't want to believe what happened was true. I was caught in the middle of making a hard decision. I had to make up my mind on what I was going to do. He was determined to recapture his loss. He wanted me back regardless of whether he hurt Steve or not. I can't help it, I tried so hard to forget about it. *(She places both hands on her chest)* It's like a knife tearing at my heart and now you. It's like our lives have been destined for suffering, all because of what war has done to our men and women and families. I know what you are going through. Steve has some symptoms like William's. Margarite, it must be really hard on Lillian.

MARGARITE: I find it hard explaining why her father is this way. I don't know when or what to say.

Zera: How about a cup of coffee or tea to calm your nerves?

MARGARITE: Tea will be fine. *(Margarite fumbles in her purse pulling out a mirror, looks at her eyes, takes out a tissue and wipes makeup from her face.)*

ZERA: I'll be right back. *(while she goes into the kitchen Margarite nervously searches in her coat pocket for cigarettes. She takes one out, lights it and looks for an ash tray. Zera returns to living room, places tray with tea on table)* Oh, I see you got up to stretch your legs.

MARGARITE: Not really, I was looking for an ash tray, I found one.

ZERA: They are hard to find around here because none of us smoke and Steve has a tendency to make them all disappear. Go ahead and finish your cigarette, girl.

MARGARITE: *(she puts out her cigarette in the ash tray)* That's alright, I can do without it. I called myself cutting down. I wasn't really aware that I had taken a drag on it.

ZERA: Nervous tension, everybody has to have something to calm their nerves. *(she pours water for tea)* What do you take in your tea?

MARGARITE: Lemon and honey, two spoons of honey will be fine.

ZERA: *(gives tea to Margarite)* And as you were saying before I left . . .

MARGARITE: Lillian doesn't know William is not her real father because Robert and I divorced when she was seven months old. The only real father she knows is William.

ZERA: I can't see anything wrong with her believing that William is her real father.

MARGARITE: It's not just that.

ZERA: *(they sit down on the sofa)* Then what is it then?

MARGARITE: Lillian has been asking me questions.

ZERA: What kind of questions?

MARGARITE: She wants to know why her Daddy yells and screams in his sleep, it frightens her. I don't want her to think he's crazy and losing his mind. If she thought that, then the affect on her would be unbearable, especially if word spread to other children at school.

ZERA: Okay, Margarite, why don't you tell her the truth while she is still young? If you wait until she is older it might cause some harsh resentment toward both you and William.

MARGARITE: I can't, she loves him so much. He is so good to her, she would rather be around him than with me at times.

ZERA: I can understand why there is so much attachment.

MARGARITE: You can?

ZERA: *(hesitates)* He loves Lillian the way he does because . . .

MARGARITE: Because what? *(pleading)* Come on Zera, tell me. I have to know.

ZERA: Because the love William is expressing to Lillian is the same love he would have expressed to . . . *(Zera stops talking to get up, walks slightly away, turns and looks at Margarite)* I can't tell you. You're having enough hardship already.

MARGARITE: *(reaching and holding Zera's hand tightly)* Tell me, please tell me, I'll be able to handle it.

ZERA: *(looking seriously into Margarite's eyes)* The love William expresses to Lillian is the same love he would have expressed to our child, *(Zera looks at the floor)* had things not turned out the way they did.

MARGARITE: Zera, you can look at me! It's not your fault or his either.

ZERA: Do you still want to tell her that William is not her real father?

MARGARITE: Robert, I thought he was the man of my dreams. Our marriage ended in divorce because of all the abuse. The only positive thing was Lillian.

ZERA: So, are you going to tell her?

MARGARITE: No! I don't want to break that bonded love they have for each other. I will tell her why he yells and does strange things in his sleep. I will explain everything to her about the war and about his being a prisoner of war.

ZERA: Do you think she'll understand?

MARGARITE: I think so, I'll have a long talk with William and he will explain to her why he's that way. *(Margarite looks at her watch and stands up)* Oh! It's almost three o'clock. I better get out of here before Lillian gets home.

ZERA: *(surprised)* Is it that late already?

MARGARITE: Yes, and I don't know where the time went. I do know if I'm not home before Lillian, she'll be over here looking for me. Plus, we know how hard it is to separate her and your son, Jahad, once they get together. I'm glad I came over, I feel better and much more relaxed now.

ZERA: *(hugs Margarite as she prepares to leave)* Yes I know, thanks for coming over Margarite. It was good therapy for both of us, we needed that. It's nice to have a friend that you can count on and talk with, in time of need for whatever reason.

MARGARITE: Thanks again, Zera. *(she closes door)*

FADE OUT

<h1 style="text-align:center"><u>SCENE V</u></h1>

ZERA IS AT HOME, CLEANING THE LIVING ROOM. JAHAD ARRIVES HOME FROM SCHOOL.

ZERA: *(hearing door open, she yells)* Jahad is that you?

STEVE: *(enters the living room as Zera walks toward the door)* I had you fooled. You thought I was Jahad arriving from school.

ZERA: Well, you did and you didn't. I was wondering why he would be arriving now, when he's not due 'til later.

STEVE: Where is he, if he's not home from school yet?

ZERA: There is no need to worry, his class went to the Staten Island Zoo today.

STEVE: Wow, you really had me concerned just then, baby. *(takes off his jacket, places it on the sofa, and they sit down)* Did I get any mail today?

ZERA: Yes, I'll get it.

STEVE: Baby, can you also bring my briefcase? I have a surprise for you.

ZERA: *(she gives him the mail and briefcase)* What is it?

STEVE: Let me take a look at my mail first. Are you nervous?

ZERA: Just a little, especially when it comes to surprises.

STEVE: Just calm down, *(he notices cigarette butts in ash tray, pointing to ash tray)* what's that?

ZERA: Oh, Margarite was here earlier.

STEVE: What was it this time?

ZERA: She was upset because William had one of those nightmares last night and she fears it will have some affect on Lillian.

STEVE: I saw William this morning at the ferry terminal and he seemed alright.

ZERA: He might have been alright then, but when Margarite called me, she was terribly upset.

STEVE: How is she now?

ZERA: She's feeling much better after talking about it.

STEVE: Zera can you get me a beer?

ZERA: *(she goes into the kitchen to get the beer from the refrigerator)* What about the surprise?

STEVE: *(he takes folder from briefcase)* I'll show it to you when you return with my beer.

ZERA: *(returns to the living room)* Honey, here's your beer.

STEVE: Thank you, Baby, *(gives Zera the plastic folder)* this is the surprise, open it.

ZERA: *(opening the folder she begins to read enclosed itinerary)* Steve this is beautiful!

STEVE: I knew you'd like it.

ZERA: I can't wait to tell Jahad. He'll be thrilled.

STEVE: You're really excited about it, aren't you? *(door opens)*

ZERA: You know I'm like a little girl when it comes to surprises.

JAHAD: *(enters arriving from school, walks toward parents)* Mommy, Daddy, what's all the excitement about? *(Zera takes his school bag and tosses it onto the sofa)* Mommy, why did you do that?

ZERA: Guess what, Jahad?

JAHAD: What Mommy?

ZERA: *(she holds Jahad's hands dancing around in a circle laughing)* Your Daddy surprised us, he's taking us to Florida to Disney World.

JAHAD: *(jumping up and down)* Wow Wee!

STEVE: Yes, Jahad, Disney World.

ZERA & JAHAD: *(singing and overjoyed)* We're on our way for a joyous time.

JAHAD: Wow Wee! Disney World. *(Jahad hugs his dad)* Thank you Daddy.

STEVE: You're welcome, Son. You and your mother both deserve a little vacation with some fun and excitement but that's not all.

ZERA: *(she sits next to Steve on the sofa, Jahad sits on his Dad's knee)* What else are you keeping from us?

STEVE: I talked it over with William and asked if we could take Lillian along.

JAHAD: *(excited)* What did he say, Daddy? Can she, is she coming with us Daddy, is she?

STEVE: All of them are coming with us. I invited the entire family.

JAHAD: *(jumps off his Dad's knee, shouting)* Wow Wee! Mickey Mouse, Minnie Mouse, Wow Wee! Disney World, Daddy? I love you Daddy.

STEVE: I love you too Son. *(Steve looks at Zera)* Why are you so quiet Zera? Did you get lost in the excitement?

ZERA: No, I was thinking how grand it would be for the kids.

STEVE: Jahad, I heard you went to the Zoo today, did you like it?

JAHAD: I liked it very much, especially the monkeys.

STEVE: Which ones? They have a variety, you know.

JAHAD: I liked the ones that look a lot like people.

STEVE: You must be talking about the chimpanzees.

JAHAD: They're the ones, they were great.

STEVE: They also have orangutans. When I was a little boy, my first time at the Zoo I enjoyed the chimps more than anything else. I also thought they looked like people. I would visualize them wearing clothes and always wanted one as a pet.

JAHAD: What happened, Daddy? Did you ever get to play with one?

STEVE: No, Jahad.

JAHAD: Daddy, tell me more.

STEVE: Jahad, the closest I came to touching a real monkey was in my squadron in Vietnam. One of my partners purchased a monkey from a young Marine who had captured it in the jungle. It was a close companion to the Marine, but he had to shoot it or let it go.

JAHAD: Why Daddy?

STEVE: Because his Platoon Sergeant was getting harassed by their Platoon Commander. Whenever the young Marine wasn't around, the monkey would go haywire and tear up everything and make a lot of noise.

JAHAD: What did the young Marine do, Daddy?

STEVE: Son, he sold it. Now tell me was there anything else you enjoyed at the Zoo?

JAHAD: I liked watching the man open the snake cage and throw in a white mouse for the snake to eat. Daddy, why do they feed the snakes white mice?

STEVE: I don't know Son.

JAHAD: The mouse wasn't even alive. There was a lot to see at the Zoo. My teacher took us to see everything. *(Jahad throws out his hand and Steve quickly reaches into his pocket as if looking for money)* Daddy give me five. Not money, Daddy, you know that thing that people do.

STEVE: Show me, Son.

JAHAD: *(they slap hands)* That's it Daddy.

STEVE: You're too much.

JAHAD: *(doorbell rings)* I'll get it Mommy!

ZERA: *(loudly)* I'll get it, Jahad. Go put your books and things in the room. *(Zera opens door)* Hello Lillian.

LILLIAN: Hello, Miss Zera, is Jahad home?

ZERA: Yes he's home, come in.

LILLIAN: *(they enter living room)* Hello, Mr. Steve.

STEVE: Hello, Lillian, how are you today?

LILLIAN: Fine, thank you, can Jahad come over to my house for a little while?

STEVE: Ask Miss Zera.

ZERA: Yes, Lillian, he can go over to your house but just for a little while?

LILLIAN: My Mother said, Jahad went to the Zoo today.

ZERA: Yes, he did.

LILLIAN: My class went last week.

ZERA: We just finished talking with Jahad about his Zoo experience. So, Lillian, what animals did you like when you went to the Zoo?

LILLIAN: I liked the reptiles.

ZERA: Have a seat, Lillian, while you wait for Jahad. He should be out in a minute.

LILLIAN: *(sits down on the sofa next to Steve)* Thank you Miss Zera.

ZERA: *(loudly)* Jahad, it's Lillian!

JAHAD: Okay Mom, I'll be right out as soon as I put on my sneakers.

ZERA: Lillian, would you like some cookies?

LILLIAN: Yes, please.

ZERA: *(exits to kitchen)* Steve, can I get you anything?

STEVE: No thanks, Dear. Lillian, did your Father get home from work yet?

LILLIAN: No, not yet, last night my Daddy was yelling again in his sleep. Mr. Steve, do you yell in your sleep and walk around and hide like my Daddy does?

STEVE: No, Lillian.

LILLIAN: I'm afraid for my Daddy. I asked Mommy if he was going crazy or going to die.

STEVE: It's nothing like that, Lillian, your Daddy is not crazy and he is not going to die.

LILLIAN: Then why is he like that?

STEVE: He's that way because of what happened to him when he was in the war.

LILLIAN: But, I love my Daddy and the war is over. I don't want him to yell and hide, and walk around in his sleep, it makes me afraid.

ZERA: *(returns to living room)* What on earth are you two talking about?

LILLIAN: We're talking about my Daddy, Miss Zera.

ZERA: Oh, did your Dad tell you about Disney World?

STEVE: *(he motions for Zera to hush and change the subject)* Zera where are the cookies?

LILLIAN: Disney World, what about Disney World?

ZERA: *(trying to keep her off the subject)* Lillian, here are your cookies.

JAHAD: *(runs out from his room)* Hi, Lillian!

LILLIAN: Hi, Jahad!

JAHAD: Lillian, did your mother tell you we are going to Disney World together?

ZERA: Jahad, would you like some cookies?

JAHAD: Yes, Mommy. *(quickly reaching for them)* Thank you, Mom. I have to finish telling Lillian about our Disney World Vacation.

STEVE: *(walks toward Zera)* Do you see what you started?

ZERA: *(walking toward kitchen)* How did I start it?

STEVE: You let the cat out of the bag with your excitement, and by telling Jahad about Disney World, that's how.

ZERA: But, what about Lillian?

STEVE: Lillian would not have known. I told William to keep it a secret, but he could tell Margarite. Now I have to call and tell him that Lillian knows already.

ZERA: Steve, I'm sorry.

STEVE: It's okay, Zera. It's not such a big thing, I was enjoying watching you and Jahad. You were like a little girl blooming with excitement, just like they are over there. I wanted to surprise Jahad by telling him on his birthday.

ZERA: Don't worry, Steve, we can still surprise him. I have planned a surprise birthday party.

JAHAD: My Mommy and Daddy told me we are going to Disney World together.

LILLIAN: My Mommy and Daddy didn't tell me anything about any Disney World.

JAHAD: Maybe they don't want you to know.

LILLIAN: But they don't keep secrets from me.

JAHAD: You never know about parents.

LILLIAN: I know mine, especially my Father, he would never lie to me.

JAHAD: Have they ever told you about the tooth fairy leaving money under your pillow when your baby teeth fall out?

LILLIAN: Yes it's true, the tooth fairy does leave money, once I got a dime.

JAHAD: You see, that's a story.

LILLIAN: *(takes Jahad's hand pulling him toward door)* Let's go to my house. My Dad should be home by now and I want to hear it from him if we are going to Disney World.

JAHAD: Lillian, wait. *(pulling her back and freeing his hand)* Why don't you believe me? Didn't my Mother and Father tell you?

LILLIAN: No. Maybe they didn't want me to know. Maybe it's some kind of surprise or something.

JAHAD: Then how come I know?

LILLIAN: You know because you're their son. Now since you know everything, tell me how are we going to get there?

JAHAD: We're going on Amtrak, that's how.

LILLIAN: That's a train!

JAHAD: I know it's a train, how else are we going to get there?

LILLIAN: Fly, haven't you heard of flying? Whoever heard of taking the train to Disney World.

JAHAD: Think about it, Lillian. Disney World, Mickey Mouse, Donald Duck, Goofy, Minnie Mouse, Snow White and the Seven Dwarfs . . .

LILLIAN: Snow White and the Seven Dwarfs! Did you say Snow White and the Seven Dwarfs?

JAHAD: Yes, Snow White and the Seven Dwarfs.

JAHAD & LILLIAN: *(Jahad and Lillian singing as they gleefully dance holding hands and circling around)* Snow White and the Seven Dwarfs, Snow White and the Seven Dwarfs, Mickey Mouse, Donald Duck and Goofy.

ZERA: *(enters living room)* What's all the excitement?

JAHAD: We are singing because I told Lillian about Disney World.

ZERA: Oh, you did? I thought you were going to Lillian's house for a little while?

LILLIAN: We are, Miss Zera.

JAHAD: Yes, Mom, we're leaving right now.

ZERA: *(happily kissing Jahad and Lillian)* Jahad make sure you're home by six.

JAHAD: Okay, Mom.

LILLIAN: *(she and Jahad leave singing and overjoyed)* Bye, Miss Zera.

___

FADE OUT

<u>SCENE VI</u>

NEXT MORNING, ZERA IS IN THE KITCHEN.

ZERA: *(wearing housecoat and slippers exits bedroom into kitchen)* Steve, Jahad, get up it's seven o'clock. *(not hearing a reply, she yells)* Steve and Jahad, get up please, I'm not calling you again!

JAHAD: *(exits bedroom to enter kitchen)* Good morning, Mommy.

ZERA: *(setting table)* Good morning, Jahad. Now what took you so long to get up this morning?

JAHAD: *(rubbing his eyes)* I was dreaming.

ZERA: Dreaming huh? Really! Well you dream right into the bathroom and get dressed, but first where is my kiss?

JAHAD: I didn't brush my teeth yet, Mommy.

ZERA: My kiss, I said I want my kiss first. *(Jahad gives her a kiss)* Now go hurry in and out of that bathroom so your father can get in there.

STEVE: *(exiting bedroom he goes into kitchen sneaking up on Zera, she does not see him)* Good morning, Baby.

ZERA: *(frightened, she drops the loaf of bread on the floor)* Now, you should know better than to sneak up on me *(she picks up the bread)* especially when I'm in the kitchen!

STEVE: Zera, I only thought I'd start the day with a little humor.

ZERA: Well Steve, I didn't think it was really funny especially this early in the morning. Where do you think you are, in 'Nam on a mission? Next time, you better make sure you know who you are sneaking up on because it could have been this *(showing him the frying pan)* up side your head.

STEVE: You're not serious, are you Zera?

ZERA: Don't I sound serious, every time I call you and Jahad in the morning to get up? I don't know how you made reveille when you were in the service. Steve please go get dressed.

STEVE: You should have been a Drill Sergeant, Zera. Why are you so hard on me this morning? You weren't like this last night.

ZERA: *(walks close to Steve giving him a kiss)* Really, Steve, do you think I'm hard on you? I'm sorry, for some reason I'm a little uptight and I don't know why. I'll just have to calm down.

JAHAD: Oh, excuse me, Mom and Dad. Mom, is it alright if I sit down to eat?

ZERA: I haven't even finished making breakfast yet, Jahad.

JAHAD: That's okay, Mom, *(pouring cereal into bowl)* I'll have cold cereal.

STEVE: I'll have the same. I'm going to the bathroom to get dressed.

ZERA: *(she sits down at table with Jahad)* What did you dream about, Disney World?

JAHAD: No. Remember what we were talking about the other day?

ZERA: Not that again.

JAHAD: It's true, Mommy, I had the same dream again. Daddy died and left us alone.

ZERA: I told you, Jahad, that your dream is not true.

JAHAD: *(showing sadness)* It's true Mommy, that's how Robbin and Cindy's parents died. They had a dream about it happening, but you promised that Daddy is not going to die.

ZERA: *(kisses him on the forehead)* Jahad be quiet, later we'll tell Daddy about your dream, okay Honey.

JAHAD: Will Daddy promise like you did?

STEVE: *(he enters kitchen)* What's all this talk about Daddy promising you? *(as Steve sits down at the kitchen table)* Do you think your Mother and I forgot your birthday?

ZERA: No Steve, it's not that, he knows we didn't forget.

STEVE: Then, what kind of secret are you two keeping from me? *(Jahad is sniffling)* Jahad, stop your sniffling. Zera, Jahad, what is it?

ZERA: *(rubbing her arms as if chilled)* He had a nightmare last night, the same one two nights in a row.

STEVE: *(looking at Jahad then back at Zera)* Okay, Son, tell me about this dream?

ZERA: Steve, I don't think he wants to tell you.

STEVE: Well, I think he should. Jahad, now tell me about your dream, Son?

ZERA: It's about you, Steve.

STEVE: What do you mean, explain to me, it's what about me? *(annoyed he hits the table with his fist)* What is it with you two? *(Steve looks at Jahad)* Well, Son, are you going to tell me?

ZERA: Steve, can't you see he is upset?

STEVE: *(hits table again with his fist)* We are all upset and I don't even know what's going on!

ZERA: It started Wednesday when he came home from school.

STEVE: Why were you upset, Son, and what does school have to do with me and your dream?

JAHAD: *(stares at his father)* Daddy, it's about Robbin and Cindy.

STEVE: Are you talking about Robbin and Cindy, the kids that I read about in the newspapers who lost their parents in a car accident?

ZERA: Yes Steve, Robbin and Cindy are the children in his class.

STEVE: I'm sorry, Son, I didn't know.

JAHAD: It's okay Daddy, but . . . *(hesitating)*

STEVE: But what, Son?

ZERA: Tell Daddy what you told me, Jahad.

JAHAD: Mommy, I'm afraid if I tell Daddy about the dream we won't get to go to Disney World.

STEVE: Is that what you are afraid of, my not taking you to Disney World? You haven't done anything wrong, Son. It's your vacation and all of us are going on this dream vacation together with the Dickensons. Doesn't that sound good to you Son? Your dream is going to come true.

JAHAD: *(crying)* No, Daddy, no. I don't want my dream to come true.

STEVE: *(looking at Zera)* I'm completely dumbfounded.

ZERA: It's not Disney World, Steve, he is afraid you are going to die and leave us alone, that's what his dream was about.

STEVE: *(looking surprised)* Look at me, Son, and listen to me good. I am not going to die and leave you and your mother alone. It was just a dream. People have dreams all the time, those dreams do not come true.

JAHAD: Then why did my friend's parents die in the car accident?

STEVE: It was meant to happen, it's called fate, Son.

ZERA: Jahad, the Lord called for them.

JAHAD: But Robbin and Cindy are alone. *(hugs his dad)* I don't want me and Mommy to be alone.

STEVE: You're not going to be alone. I'm going to be right here with you and your mother, and you know what else? I'm going to pick up your birthday cake today so we can celebrate your seventh birthday. Now, how does that sound?

JAHAD: But, Daddy, promise me you won't die and leave me and Mommy here alone.

STEVE: Look Son, see *(crossing his heart)* I'm crossing my heart. Go ahead, Zera, cross your heart also. See, we crossed our hearts and promise not to die and leave you alone, okay?

ZERA: Now please can we eat, so that you two can get out of here before you are late.

JAHAD: *(he finishes eating and gets up from table)* Excuse me, Mom and DAD.

ZERA & STEVE: You're excused Son.

JAHAD: Thank you, Mommy and Daddy.

STEVE: Jahad, what Disney character do you want on your cake?

JAHAD: Goofy, Daddy, Goofy.

STEVE: You got it, Son, I'll bring it this evening after work. *(Jahad walks away smiling, Steve smiles)* You know something Zera? We're a fantastic family just like old times.

ZERA: No, it's not like old times. We are living for now or did you forget? The past is forgotten. It's really great, how you and William get along, and how nice of you to invite them on our vacation. I feel like they are family.

STEVE: We are family, a family of real close friends raising beautiful children.

ZERA: I'm going to call Margarite and ask her to pick up Jahad after school. Maybe she can take him to a movie with Lillian so I can get things ready for his birthday celebration. I sent out invitations over two weeks ago.

STEVE: That is fantastic, Zera. I know he will be surprised when Margarite brings him home and he finds the house filled with excitement. He deserves it, I'm so proud of our son. I can imagine the expression on his face. You don't think Lillian told him anything do you?

ZERA: Lillian doesn't know. I only told Margarite.

STEVE: Well, you know how kids talk when they get together.

ZERA: Everything will be okay, Steve.

STEVE: *(looking at his watch)* I better get myself together so I can get out of here. *(kisses Zera)* I'll see you later this evening.

ZERA: Okay, Honey, have a good day.

STEVE: You too, Baby. *(he leaves)*

ZERA: *(calls Margarite on the telephone)* Hello, Margarite. I want to know if you can pick up Jahad from school today? *(pause)* Remember, today is the surprise birthday celebration. *(pause)* You're taking them to a movie and McDonald's sounds great.

(pause) No, he won't suspect a thing. *(pause)* He just knows his Dad is bringing him a birthday cake. *(pause)* Thanks, Marge, I'll see you later.

FADE OUT

<u>SCENE VII</u>

BIRTHDAY CELEBRATION

ZERA: *(knock on door)* Who is it?

BARBARA: It's me, Barbara, surprise!

ZERA: *(opens door)* Oh, hi Barbara *(pause)* why are you alone? Where are your brother's children? I thought you said you were bringing them with you.

BARBARA: I did say that, but I guess I anticipated. My brother called me this morning, and said he was out of town and the children had a conflict. That's the reason why they are not with me. It's been a long time since I was here. Anyway Zera, how have you been? Can I come in?

ZERA: Oh, of course, I'm sorry. Please come in and sit down. I'm fine thank you. Can I offer you anything, coffee, tea, juice, wine?

BARBARA: A little wine, please.

ZERA: *(knock at door)* Excuse me, Barbara, please make yourself at home. *(Barbara pours glass of wine while Zera answers door)* Hello Mildred, I was hoping it was you.

MILDRED: What's happening girl? You seem so surprised.

ZERA: I am, I thought you were bringing your neighbor's kids for Jahad's birthday celebration.

MILDRED: I called my neighbor this morning, she said the kids were sick with the flu and could not come. So, anyway, here I am.

ZERA: Well, come on in.

BARBARA: Well, well, well. Look what the wind blew in, Mrs. Mildred Anson.

MILDRED: That's right, and how are you?

BARBARA: I'm okay. I'm here for Jahad's surprise birthday celebration.

ZERA: Mildred, why don't you join Barbara and me in a glass of wine?

MILDRED: Okay. *(Zera gets the wine. Mildred sits at table with Barbara)*

BARBARA: Mildred I saw you the other week with three girls and two boys, I'm surprised you didn't bring them with you.

MILDRED: They were my sister's three girls and my neighbor's two boys.

BARBARA: I didn't think they were all your's since you recently tied the knot. *(Zera sipping wine and listening)*

ZERA: *(telephone rings)* Hello! *(pause)* Okay Marg, I'll get everything ready. I'll hide everything and turn down the lights. *(pause)* Steve didn't arrive yet with the cake, he's late. I'll tell Jahad not to worry about the cake because I know his father won't forget to get it. *(pause)* Just give me about five minutes to get everything together. *(pause)* Okay, see you in a few. *(end of call)*

Mildred, Barbara, I need you to help me quickly. Margarite is on her way, she's bringing Jahad and Lillian upstairs.

BARBARA: Oh, it's Lillian's birthday, too?

ZERA: No, I asked Margarite if she would pick up Jahad from school when she picked up Lillian. I didn't want him here when everyone arrived. I really wanted everything to be a surprise. *(there's a knock on the door)* Excuse me while I let them in.

JAHAD: Hi Mommy, did Daddy get home with the cake? I want Miss Margarite and Lillian to have some, they took me to the movies and McDonald's for my birthday.

ZERA: Daddy hasn't come home yet. I'm still waiting for him to arrive with the cake. Did you thank Miss Margarite and Lillian for the nice time?

JAHAD: *(turns to Lillian and Miss Margarite)* Thank you, Miss Margarite and Lillian.

MARGARITE: You're welcome, Jahad.

LILLIAN: We did it because we love you and because it was our birthday gift to you.

ZERA: Jahad, Miss Barbara and Miss Mildred are here to celebrate with us and they have gifts for you also.

———

FADE OUT

SCENE VIII

NEWSPAPER STAND, CORNER OF (42nd St./8th Ave., NYC)

NEWSPAPER MAN: Sir! Can I help you with anything?

WILLIAM: I'm trying to decide whether to buy the Jet or the Ebony Magazine. I can't remember which one my wife subscribes to, I'm trying to think.

NEWSPAPER MAN: I have all of them, Ebony, Jet, Black Stars, Tan and WWRL Soul Publications. Also I have the Amsterdam News, which you usually don't find at other newspaper stands around here. Why don't you call her?

WILLIAM: Sounds good *(pause, thinking)* now I remember from last week's cover, it was the Jet Magazine. I remember now because it was the little one. So, how's business today?

NEWSPAPER MAN: Business could be a lot better, but with all the hoodlums on the streets and in the subways, it's running the customers away. Times Square or should I say 42nd Street is known throughout the world as the happening place to be. If people really knew what kind of jungle this place is, it reminds me of when I fought in the war. No matter how you look at it, whether at home or abroad it's still a war. You see, that's why I carry this *(he shows William a concealed gun)*, and hope that I don't have to use it.

FADE OUT

SCENE IX

STEVE, CARRYING HIS BRIEFCASE, APPROACHES THE STAIRS OF THE SUBWAY STATION (42nd St./8th Ave., NYC)

STEVE: *(he sees William and he walks up behind him)* Mister, can you spare any loose change? *(William ignores him)* Mister, can you spare a nickel or a dime?

WILLIAM: *(takes coins from his pants pocket and turns with hand extended)* Here! *(realizing it's Steve)* What in the hell kind of trick was that?

STEVE: I just thought I would surprise you.

WILLIAM: This isn't the place for surprises, 42nd Street and Vietnam. This place gives me the creeps. *(he looks around)* It's just like the jungles of Southeast Asia. You never know when your time is up.

STEVE: *(playfully hitting William on the shoulder with his fist)* What in the hell are you doing up here on 42nd Street?

WILLIAM: *(scratching his chin)* I'm getting off from work the same as you.

STEVE: *(smiling)* I'm surprised to see you in this area.

WILLIAM: I just came from work and had to make a stop before heading home. *(looking at his watch)* You're kind of late yourself, aren't you?

STEVE: I figured I'd leave the job a little late. I have to pick up my son's birthday cake at the Sugar and Bun Cake Shop.

WILLIAM: *(nodding his head in agreement)* That's right, I knew it was something. Margarite had mentioned it to me last week. *(rubs his brow)* I have to stop and pick up something for your son.

STEVE: William, you don't have to.

WILLIAM: I want to because your little man is just like a brother to Lillian, and a son to Margarite and me.

STEVE: Give me five. *(he extends his hand, William slaps it and they make a tight handshake)*

WILLIAM: What we have here is a solid friendship, especially considering what I tried to do to you years ago.

STEVE: Hey man, forget it, that's all in the past. I don't fault you, I forgave you. What happened was all because of the messed up war.

WILLIAM: Thanks, man. *(he looks down for a moment)* I don't know what to say, except life is like two ships on the ocean passing in opposite directions never to pass again. It is the same with people. This is why it is important to open up lines of communication because you will never know how many lives you can touch for the betterment of mankind. It is the humanitarian thing to do.

STEVE: Let's just say that somewhere in our lifetime we've all been faced with hard decisions, choices, and challenges. It's all part of life. Many of those who came back from Vietnam are homeless or suffering with a multitude of health issues and disorders. I guess we are lucky. The fight never ended, it still continues especially when it comes to getting help and veterans benefits.

WILLIAM: Steve if you ever need a friend, you know, to cover you in a jungle or war on the streets you can always count on me. I got your back.

STEVE: You can count on me too, man. *(looks at his watch)* It's 7:30pm, we better pick up what we have to get and head for home before our wives start to worry.

WILLIAM: Yeah, especially mine, because I usually call her when I think I'll be a little late.

STEVE: I bet Lillian worries, too.

WILLIAM: Yes, she does.

STEVE: She's one kind, sweet, cute, intelligent little girl. What kind of reaction did you get when you told her we would be going to Disney World together?

WILLIAM: You wouldn't believe it, Steve. *(scratches his head)* It was like she knew already.

STEVE: She did, Zera told Jahad when he came in from school, and then he completely blew it in front of Lillian.

WILLIAM: Margarite and Lillian's reaction sure had me puzzled. I just couldn't understand why Lillian was so calm while Margarite was bursting full of excitement.

STEVE: Zera was the same way, but I enjoyed every moment of their excitement. *(Steve reminisces in a stare)* It brought back my childhood memories of going to the Roy Rogers Wild West Rodeo Show at the old Madison Square Garden. I went with our neighbors who also took their children.

WILLIAM: I know what you mean, I have some good memories like that also. Man, we need to get going, which train are you taking?

STEVE: I'm taking the A train down to Chambers, then head down to South Ferry.

WILLIAM: While you pick up the cake, I'll stop at the store next to the newspaper stand and pick up your son's present. Then I'll meet you on the A, downtown platform. *(he looks at his watch)* How about in fifteen minutes?

STEVE: Okay. That's cool.

WILLIAM: *(they exit in different directions)* See you in a few.

———

FADE OUT

<u>SCENE</u> X

UNDERGROUND PASSAGEWAY TO SUBWAY PLATFORM, UPTOWN / DOWNTOWN (A) AND (E) TRAINS.

STEVE: *(walking through passageway carrying briefcase and cake box, seeking directions)* Excuse me, young man, but is this the passageway to the downtown train?

WEASEL: Yeah, man, only I think you're a little early because I didn't hear your train. *(looking at his gang members standing nearby)* Did you hear this man's train?

MONKEY: Mister, you're in the wrong place at the wrong time. *(Monkey, mimicking and dancing around, takes off his belt)*

STEVE: You should leave your belt on, it looks good on you.

MONKEY: What! You're a wise guy? You know who you talking to? *(pointing to himself with his thumb)*

JOSH: *(pointing to Monkey)* He's Monkey, man, Monkey. *(Josh does monkey antics)*

MONKEY: Yeah! I'm Monkey and if you talk outta your face *(pointing to Steve's face)* I'm going to "monkey" all over you man. *(Monkey nodding his head up and down because Steve does not answer)* You hear me, man?

NATE: *(pushing Steve's shoulder)* You hear Monkey talking to you, man?

JOSH: *(pushes Steve)* When Monkey's talking everybody listens.

JULIO: Don't push him so hard, man, he looks like a punk. *(Josh pushes Steve again)*

WEASEL: He could be "the man," a decoy maybe!

JOSH: *(pushing Steve again and again)* Are you "the man," man?

STEVE: No, I'm not the man, just an ordinary citizen.

JOSH: *(turns and looks at his comrades)* You hear that fellas? *(laughing at Monkey jumping and doing monkey tantrums)* He's not the man, just a citizen like us.

WEASEL: Hey, Josh! I think you got Monkey started. *(Weasel goes to Monkey)* Hey! Monkey, cool it down.

NATE: Look what we got here, *(snapping his fingers and walking around Steve)* this man is clean.

JOSH: *(looking at Steve's clothes, circles him and feels the fabric)* Maybe he's a pimp.

NATE: If he's a pimp, what's he doing taking the iron horse? Can you believe it? He's dressed like that wearing Italian silk or is it shark skin, riding the iron horse with ordinary citizens like us.

MONKEY: *(Josh and Monkey laugh)* Maybe his pimpmobile got repossessed by the IRS.

WEASEL: *(looks at Steve's shoes, then looks at his own sneakers)* Hey! I dig my man's shoes. They look like my size, maybe I should trade mine in.

JULIO: *(looking at Weasel)* Maybe they are your size. *(speaking to Steve)* Hey, mister, how's about letting my man Weasel try on your shoes? If they fit he keeps them, *(Steve looks hard at Julio)* and you get to keep his sneakers.

STEVE: Fellas, what is it you want? I'm not asking for trouble.

MONKEY: Did you hear that, fellas? *(as he's poking Steve's chest with his finger)* This clean super stud don't want no trouble.

STEVE: *(pleading)* Please fellas, I said, I'm not looking for trouble. All I want to do is catch my train and go home.

JULIO: Hey, man, you don't tell us what you want!

NATE: Yeah! Can't you see, *(Nate sticks out his chest)* we're in charge, we tell you what to do.

WEASEL: We're in charge and don't care whether you like it or not, got that buddy.

JOSH: *(snatches cake box from Steve)* Give me that box.

WEASEL: *(takes briefcase)* Let's open the box? Maybe there are some cookies or cake inside *(rubbing his stomach)* hell, I'm hungry.

JOSH: *(to Steve)* Hey, man! *(Josh takes out a pocket knife to cut the string on the box)* What's in the box?

STEVE: I'm asking you please don't open the box, it's for my son, it's his birthday.

JULIO: *(pushes Steve)* What did I tell you before? You don't hear too well, do you? You don't tell us nothing, man. Shut your face or I'll shut it for you.

WEASEL: Hey Josh, open up the box man. I said, I'm hungry.

JOSH: *(to Weasal)* Who got the box, you or me?

WEASEL: You got it, man.

JOSH: So, just wait until I get ready to open it.

NATE: Wait a minute, man, who put you in charge? We're all in this together.

JOSH: We're all in charge.

MONKEY: Yeah! So whatever goes down or comes from that ever loving damn box, briefcase case, his wallet, his pockets or his clothes, down to his damn underwear, we splits. *(he points to Steve)* I say we splits it right down the middle, agree?

NATE & JOSH: We agree.

WEASEL: Me too.

MONKEY: Well, Julio, what about you? *(Julio not answering)* Well, Julio, *(all of them look at him. Monkey goes over to Julio and shoves him)* are you with us?

JULIO: Man, what the heck's wrong with you? Are you crazy?

MONKEY: Julio, you going to be a bastard all your damn life? *(Julio gives Monkey a hard stare)* Wake up Julio and smell the roses, man are you with us or not?

JULIO: Yeah! But you didn't have to push me.

MONKEY: Good! So now we all agree. *(Monkey fidgeting with his hands and looks at Steve)* We going to take my man, and if one of us goes down we all go down together.

STEVE: *(throws up his hands)* Cool it, fellas, I'm not looking for a fight.

WEASEL: Who said anything about a fight, chump!

JULIO: I'm tired of you, I'm tired of looking at you, *(Julio pushes Steve and Steve grabs him and throws him down on the ground. All of Julio's partners go to aid him. They pull Steve off of Julio and separate them)* I'm tired of you coming outta your face.

WEASEL: Cool it, Julio, are you mad? *(struggling with Julio)*

MONKEY: We aren't looking for a fight.

STEVE: *(yelling in anger)* You are all just a bunch of punks with no respect for yourselves or anybody else.

NATE: The man is right, why don't we cool it?

MONKEY: What are you doing, taking sides? There won't be no cooling it I said, the man is out of bounds.

STEVE: Out of bounds?

MONKEY: Yeah! *(pointing at Steve)* You heard me, out of bounds, just by you being here is considered out of bounds for citizens like you.

STEVE: You are nothing but a bunch of ill-rated has-beens. You're not worth the nine months of pain your mothers suffered carrying you little devil bastards into this world.

NATE: Oh, so we're bastards now?

STEVE: You're worse than that.

NATE: *(in Steve's face)* yo, man, I tried to cool my boys down and talk some sense into them, but *(pushing Steve)* I don't like the way you just came outta your face.

STEVE: Look, I told you, I'm not a fighter. None of you are worth a damn, and you're just like them.

NATE: I'm not like them.

STEVE: You're with them, aren't you? You agreed when you said, all of you would go down together.

MONKEY: *(yells at Nate)* What you going to do, Nate, let that chump soften you up?

NATE: *(looks at Monkey)* No, man, I'm not turning soft. *(pokes Steve with his finger)* They're my boys, we are like family and whatever goes down, I go with them.

WEASEL: *(the rest of the gang members are watching as Julio cuts the string from the cake box)* Hey Nate, come on over, we are going to open up the cake box.

NATE: *(motions, pointing to Steve)* Hey you, *(Steve looks at him)* with the suit and the shoes.

WEASEL: *(looks at Steve's shoes)* Those are my shoes Nate, he's just wearing them for now.

MONKEY: *(pats Weasel on the back)* I know, man, we are going to get some of my man's duds.

JULIO: Listen up, mister, why don't we have a guessing game of what's in the box and whoever is right gets to keep it?

MONKEY: Forget it, Julio, not when food is involved.

JULIO: *(turns to Steve)* Hey, chump, *(Steve does not answer)* what's in the box?

JOSH: Maybe we got ourselves a birthday cake.

NATE: How do you know it's a cake?

JOSH: It's in a cake box, dummy, isn't it?

NATE: *(pushes Josh)* Watch your mouth, man, I'm not a dummy.

JOSH: Man, can't you take a joke?

NATE: I'm serious, man, serious.

WEASEL: Maybe it's a cake for his girl.

JOSH: Hey, Weasel, man, maybe it's cookies or Jewish pastry.

WEASEL: Kosher, man, Kosher.

JULIO: *(shaking the box)* Yeah! Maybe we got ourselves some kosher cookies.

WEASEL: No, man, don't shake it, if it's cookies they will crumble.

JULIO: Yeah! Okay I understand what you mean. Maybe he's bringing cookies home to his girl to get to her cookie.

MONKEY: Not cookie, man, peep hole.

JULIO: *(scratches his head)* Peep hole? What's that?

Monkey: Man, come on, you know you're from the block aren't you? Julio, just open the box.

STEVE: No! *(surrounded by gang members, he yells angrily)* Please!

MONKEY: And why shouldn't we?

STEVE: It's my son's birthday cake.

JULIO: Well that's too bad, mister.

WEASEL: Yeah, we like cake.

JOSH: We're hungry and we are going to eat every crumb.

MONKEY: Open up the damn box. *(Julio opens up the box and starts laughing)* What's so funny?

NATE: What is it?

JULIO: It's a birthday cake to Jahad with a picture of Goofy.

MONKEY: *(looking in the box)* Jahad, *(starts laughing)* Who the hell is Jahad?

WEASEL: *(laughs)* Maybe he's some Arab or Muslim Sheik.

JOSH: He could be related to that wrestler the Iron Sheik or Sadat or Arafat.

MONKEY: *(asks Steve)* Hey, man, you want some of Julio's birthday cake?

STEVE: *(steps toward Julio but stops)* You punks are messing up my son's birthday cake.

WEASEL: *(rips out a piece of cake and starts eating it)* That's too bad, mister, this cake belongs to Julio. Right guys?

THE GANG: Yeah!

MONKEY: Maybe the chump wants a piece of Julio's cake. How about it, chump, would you like a piece of Julio's cake?

STEVE: You guys are going to pay. You ruined my son's birthday cake, you brainless bastards!

MONKEY: Aw, gee, fellas, we have ruined Jahad's cake and my man looks mad, doesn't he?

STEVE: I promised my son a birthday cake.

NATE: *(looking at Steve)* Well, that's just too bad, mister.

JOSH: *(speaking to Steve)* Hey, chump! You can tell Jahad you celebrated with us, Julio and the boys.

WEASEL: Yeah! That's right.

JOSH: It's Julio's birthday, too. So we thought we would celebrate Julio's birthday first. *(pats Julio on the back)* Right, Julio?

JULIO: *(doesn't answer, looking starry-eyed remembering his childhood, he yells)* I can't take it, I can't stand it!

MONKEY: Can't stand what?

JULIO: *(pointing at Steve)* Him, that rat bastard who keeps talking outta his face. I'm going to shut him up.

NATE: Yeah, Julio, that's what he needs.

WEASEL: Give him a piece of your cake.

JOSH: Hey, wait a minute. I want some too.

JULIO: *(snatches a piece of cake from the box, walks over to Steve)* I'm sick and tired of hearing you. *(smashes cake into Steve's mouth)* Eat this for your son.

MONKEY: Hey y'all, we got to stop Julio before someone gets hurt. *(He and Weasel try to subdue Julio who is irrational, Steve and Julio tussle. The gang members separate them, Monkey and Weasel grab Julio while Josh and Nate hold Steve)*

JULIO: *(hysterically upset, crying and trying to talk)* A birthday cake, I never celebrated a birthday in my whole life. My mother was raped, that's why I am here. I didn't ask to be born. If I ever find out who my old man is, I'll kill the bastard. It's because of him I spent twenty-one years of my life in orphanages, reform schools, detention houses, and on the streets. I never knew my father. *(Julio pulls out a knife from his pocket and struggles with Monkey and Weasel. They attempt to hold him back from attacking Steve with the knife)*

MONKEY: Julio, cool it! You can't blame this man for what someone did to your mother.

JULIO: I don't care. *(Julio breaks loose and lunges toward Steve with the knife. Steve breaks away from Josh and Nate and side steps moving out of the way. Nate, standing behind Steve, is accidentally stabbed in his left arm and collapses. Josh grabs Steve but he cannot contain him. Julio quickly removes the knife from Nate and stabs Steve in the chest. As he pulls the knife out, Steve falls to the ground.)*

MONKEY: *(he and Weasel yelling)* Julio, man, look what you've done. You stabbed a man and you don't even know him.

JULIO: *(holding knife in his hand)* I had to do it man. I had to kill him. He didn't deserve to live. *(crying)* Nobody ever gave a damn about me. My whole life has been nothing but chaos and drama. I don't have any family or anyone to go to. I'm just tired of this whole rat race.

JOSH: Julio, you stabbed Nate, also. Why? Get rid of the knife. Give it to me. *(Josh takes the knife)*

JULIO: He made me do it. *(pointing to Steve on the ground)* He made me do it man!

MONKEY: *(speaking out)* Come on you guys, let's get the hell out of here. Help me with Nate, that goes for you to Julio. *(Monkey looking in the distance)* I think those people saw us. *(as they leave the scene running, trying to find the nearest exit, Josh throws the knife into a garbage bin. Weasel, decides to go back)* Weasel, where you going man?

WEASEL: I'll be right back. I have to get something. It won't take long. I'll catch up to you.

WILLIAM: *(returns to meet Steve on the platform, seeing the cake box next to Steve on the ground, and Weasel bending down beside him, William yells fiercely)* Hey man! What the hell are you doing? *(he sees Weasel remove and take Steve's shoes and briefcase. As Weasel runs away, his wallet drops out of his pocket. William approaching Steve)* No! No! No!

STEVE: *(tries to speak)* I'm sorry, man.

WILLIAM: *(bends down to cradle Steve's head in his arms,)* Don't talk, I'll get help.

STEVE: *(gasping for air and coughing up blood)* I won't need any.

WILLIAM: Please, man, don't die on me. It's your son's birthday.

STEVE: I know, and I promised him a birthday cake.

WILLIAM: You're my best friend. We've been through hell in the war. I love you like a brother.

STEVE: I know but . . . William, tell Jahad and Zera I am sorry. I, I, broke my promise. *(his eyelids close, he dies)*

WILLIAM: *(crying while holding Steve)* You bastards, you punk bastards, no, not my man Steve, they will pay, every punk I run into. Steve, I promise. *(resting Steve's head on the ground, he picks up the wallet and looks through it)* Weasel . . . I got you, Weasel. I know you are out there. You can run but you can't hide. You will pay for what you did to my friend and his family. Nobody will know, nobody but me. *(Weasel, realizing he doesn't have his wallet, Weasel runs back to the scene and sees William holding it. Tackling him to the ground, Weasel pulls out a knife and stabs William several times. Hearing voices in the distance, Weasel panics and runs from the scene.)*

FADE OUT

<u>SCENE XI</u>

9:30PM, BIRTHDAY CELEBRATION, ZERA AND JAHAD AT HOME WITH GUESTS AWAITING STEVE.

BARBARA: Zera, here comes your son, Jahad.

MILDRED: He looks upset.

MARGARITE: He has reason to be, this is supposed to be his surprise birthday party.

ZERA: It's not much of a surprise anymore because his dad is late. *(concerned)* I wonder what is keeping him? Let me see what time it is. *(looking at clock)* It can't be that late, can it?

BARBARA: Yeah, honey, it's almost ten o'clock.

MARGARITE: Maybe the cake wasn't ready.

ZERA: He would have called to let me know something.

MILDRED: Maybe he is working late.

ZERA: No way, Mildred, Steve would never break his promise to Jahad by having him wait like this.

BARBARA: Don't worry, Zera, I bet he is on his way home right now but stopped to pick up another surprise for your son.

ZERA: Not Steve at this hour, if anyone knows him well, it is me. *(rubbing her hands together)* I hope he gets here soon because he has everyone worried and waiting.

JAHAD: *(goes to table, Zera slides her chair back and sits him on her lap)* Mommy, Daddy promised to bring my cake.

ZERA: I know, Son. Mommy is wondering, too. Your Dad should have been home a long time ago.

MILDRED: *(tries to change the subject)* He's so cute, he is the spitting image of Steve.

BARBARA: Yeah, I do see the similarities.

MARGARITE: Well, girls, you know how it is *(smiling)* you can't have everything.

JAHAD: *(there is a heavy knock on the door, Jahad excited jumps off his mother's lap)* Mommy, it's Daddy with the cake.

ZERA: Jahad *(pause)*

JAHAD: *(running toward the door)* I'll get it Mommy. *(he opens the door)* Hello Officer *(pause)*

POLICE OFFICER: Hello, Son, is your mother at home?

JAHAD: Yes, Sir *(pause)*

ZERA: *(yells out)* Jahad, who is it?

JAHAD: It's a policeman with the cake, Mommy.

ZERA: *(goes to the door)* I know it's your birthday party but it isn't the time for your Dad to make a joke at this late hour especially after keeping everyone waiting.

POLICE OFFICER: *(looking at Zera, motioning for her to send her son away)* Ma'am, would you . . . ?

JAHAD: Where is my Daddy?

ZERA: Jahad, would you please take yourself into your room.

JAHAD: But where is my Daddy?

ZERA: Jahad, please do as you are told, now go.

MARGARITE: Excuse me, girls, I'm going to see what this is about. *(very concerned, goes to door to accompany Zera)*

MILDRED: Yes, please, and come back and let us know.

BARBARA: *(talking to Mildred)* I'm going to pour myself another drink.

MARGARITE: What is wrong, Officer?

POLICE OFFICER: Which one of you ladies is Mrs. Rogers?

ZERA: I am, Sir.

POLICE OFFICER: I'm sorry, Miss, but I'm afraid I have some bad news. *(he holds out a cake box and shopping bag. Zera breaks down crying profoundly with hands covering her face, almost faints)*

BARBARA: *(becomes excited hearing Zera crying)* Mildred, Mildred! *(Barbara and Mildred rush to the door. They take the bag and cake box and place them on the living room table).*

POLICE OFFICER: *(to Margarite)* Excuse me Miss, would you please help me to get Mrs. Rogers over to the sofa to sit down.

BARBARA: *(to Mildred)* Girl, from the way things look and the way the Officer came in, *(shaking her head)* looks like some really bad news.

MILDRED: I hate times like this.

BARBARA: I think I really need to sit down.

MILDRED: I'm not prepared for this.

POLICE OFFICER: *(as Zera gains control of herself, the Police Officer hesitantly)* Mrs. Rogers, I'm sorry, but . . .

ZERA: *(looking up and crying)* No! No! Not my husband, please Lord, not Steve.

POLICE OFFICER: Yes, ma'am, your husband.

ZERA: Oh God, no, Please, Lord, not Steve. *(looks at the officer, pleading)* Tell me nothing serious has happened to my husband, *(crying hysterically)* PLEASE!

MARGARITE: *(begins sobbing)* Oh God, I can't believe this. *(she wipes Zera's eyes)* Zera, I can't believe this is happening.

POLICE OFFICER: Ma'am, Mrs. Rogers, your husband was mugged and killed in the 42nd Street Subway Station. *(Zera cries harder and rocks back and forth. Shaking her head, she screams and grabs her stomach, and looks at Margarite)* We don't know what the motive was, but we were able to trace your husband to this address from the cake box receipt. The only lead we have come up with is a name, Weasel, and that could be an alias. *(Police Officer to Margarite)* Ma'am, you will find the remainder of the cake in the box. The bag has an unopened gift in it. This is all of the information I have for now, I'm sorry for your loss. I'm going to leave but someone from our precinct will be getting in touch with you.

MARGARITE: Thank you, Sir. I'll walk with you to the door. *(she returns to the living room and sits down to comfort Zera)* Zera, I'm so sorry.

LILLIAN: Jahad, I hear our mothers crying.

JAHAD: What Lillian?

LILLIAN: I think everyone is crying.

JAHAD: Let's go see! *(exiting bedroom he takes Lillian by the hand, they enter living room and walk toward their mothers seated on the sofa)* Mommy, why is everybody crying?

LILLIAN: Mommy, what's wrong?

ZERA: *(extending her hand to Jahad)* Come to me Jahad. *(pausing to get the words out)* Jahad, your Daddy is dead.

JAHAD: *(pulling away, crying and stomping his feet)* No! Not my Daddy!

LILLIAN: *(shaking her mother and crying)* Mommy, that's not true is it, not Uncle Steve, right, Mommy?

MARGARITE: *(crying)* Yes, Lillian, Uncle Steve is dead. He was killed by a mugger.

JAHAD: *(jumping furiously)* Mommy, Mommy, not my Daddy. *(crying)* Daddy, Daddy, you promised, you promised me.

MARGARITE: *(reaches for Lillian, hugging her)* Lillian, I don't know how I'm going to break this news to your father.

BARBARA: Mildred, I think I'm going to leave.

MILDRED: I guess I should go also.

BARBARA: Zera, we are so very sorry. It's hard for us to put into words. Our hearts ache so much for you and Jahad. We're going to leave. You have our phone numbers, if there is anything we can do, please call. *(Barbara and Mildred both kiss Zera, then exit the apartment)*

MARGARITE: Zera, I know you and Jahad will need some time for yourselves. I need to get Lillian home. It's late and we haven't heard anything from William. If you need me for anything at all, call me. *(as they prepare to leave Margarite and Lillian embrace Jahad and Zera)*

FADE OUT

SCENE XII

EARLY A.M. HOURS, POLICE OFFICER ARRIVES AT THE HOME OF MARGARITE.

POLICE OFFICER: *(Margarite opening the door)* Pardon me Ma'am but are you Mrs. William Dickenson?

MARGARITE: Yes, Officer, I saw you several hours ago at my neighbor's apartment.

POLICE OFFICER: Is your husband Mr. William Dickenson?

MARGARITE: Yes he is, and I don't know why he is not home yet. I've called everywhere. My daughter and I are absolutely hysterical.

POLICE OFFICER: I have his I.D. Ma'am.

MARGARITE: *(looking at the officer strangely)* What, you have what?

POLICE OFFICER: Ma'am I have some other bad news. Your husband was also killed.

MARGARITE: *(yelling and crying)* My husband, oh no, not my husband, too. Lillian, Lillian come here. *(child runs out from bedroom and hugs her mother)*

POLICE OFFICER: I am terribly sorry to be the one to deliver this tragic news. I think Mr. Dickenson was killed while helping Mr. Rogers in the passageway of the 8th Avenue/42nd Street Subway Station. I really don't have any other information, but I do know you will need to go to the County Morgue to identify his body as soon as possible.

MARGARITE: Officer, can't you please, at least, tell me how it happened?

POLICE OFFICER: The only thing that we have to go on is what I mentioned to you. We won't know the details until we have a thorough investigation. Maybe you can contact Mrs. Rogers and the two of you can go together.

MARGARITE: *(as officer leaves)* Thank you, Officer, I will get myself together as soon as possible. *(Margarite crying, goes to the telephone and dials Zera's number)*

ZERA: *(telephone rings and she answers the phone)* Hello, *(hears crying)* Margarite is that you? Why are you yelling and crying. *(hesitant)* What?

MARGARITE: Zera, William is gone. William is dead. The Police just left, they think it may have had something to do with Steve. I need to go to the Morgue with you and begin funeral arrangements.

FADE OUT

SCENE XIII

FUNERAL SERVICE CONDUCTED BY ASSISTANT PASTOR JAMES HUDD (SERVICE BEGINS WITH CONGREGATION SINGING, READING OF SCRIPTURES, AND TESTIMONIALS BY FAMILY AND FRIENDS).

ASSISTANT PASTOR HUDD: Brothers and Sisters can we please observe a minute of silence for our fallen heroes (*pause for minute of silence*) Thank you, I have been asked by both families to render this Home-Going service today. I am James Hudd, Assistant Pastor to Reverend Mitchell, who could not be here today. Due to the friendship of these men, the families have requested that their funeral services be conducted together. I will now deliver the eulogy.

It is with deep regret that we are gathered here today in sympathy, with the bereaved families of our late dear Brothers Steve Rogers, and William Dickenson, former comrades and prisoner-of-war veterans of the Vietnam War.

This is a sad occasion because the deaths of these two men didn't occur in the war. They occurred right here at home in our very own backyard of the concrete jungle.

They were caused by those who roam the streets and subways, preying upon innocent people. These lost souls are roaming around everywhere because they have nothing else to do. They have no respect for life or themselves because they have no fear of God. They are filled with the devil and allow Satan to control their lives.

There's no need for me to say anymore. We're here paying our respects to these two families, especially the lovely wives Sister Margarite Dickenson and their daughter, Lillian, and our Sister Zera Rogers and their son, Jahad.

We want these families to know that they have our total support and if there's anything we can do, please, do not hesitate to let us know. The Lord gave me the honor to know both Steve and William. They were real family men. They have touched many hearts and lives. They have shown true love and respect for their fellow brothers and sisters. They would not want us to grieve. They would want us to go on with our lives, and prepare ourselves for that time when we, too, will be called upon.

With all the love they both shared in life with all of us, their spirit will continue to live on in the hearts of many. They were called upon by God, for He has work for them to do in his vineyard. He sent his angels to lift Brothers Steve Rogers and William Dickenson up through the pearly gates of eternal life, where they will be rewarded in heavenly glory.

In Jesus name, Amen

Now I'd like to ask all of you to please stand. *(folded American Flags are presented to Zera and Margarite by Pastor Hudd, himself a former military veteran)*

As the officiating clergy and on behalf of the families, I want to thank all of you for your presence here today. This concludes the Home-Going service of Brothers Steve Rogers and William Dickenson. The families ask that you join them for the burial that will take place at the Frederick Douglass Cemetery, here on Staten Island. Everyone please, stand, let us pray.

FADE OUT

<u>SCENE XIV</u>

A FEW MONTHS LATER, ROBERT, LILLIAN'S BIOLIGICAL FATHER APPEARS UNEXPECTEDLY AT MARGARITE'S HOME TO SEE HIS DAUGHTER.

LILLIAN: Mommy, somebody's knocking at the door.

MARGARITE: Are you sure Lillian? I didn't hear anything.

LILLIAN: *(another knock)* There it is again Mommy. Do you want me to see who it is?

MARGARITE: *(reading the newspaper)* Yes, please see who it is, dear.

LILLIAN: *(walking toward the door)* Who is it?

ROBERT: Delivery! I have a delivery, a package for a Miss Lillian Brown. Is she at home?

LILLIAN: Yes, *(Lillian opens the door and sees a man holding a package)* I am Lillian Brown *(pause)* Dickenson.

ROBERT: *(gives her the package)* This is for you.

LILLIAN: *(she accepts it)* What is it, who's it from?

ROBERT: *(he smiles)* It's from your father, Robert Brown.

LILLIAN: My father?

ROBERT: Lillian, didn't your mother ever tell you about me? I'm your father, Robert Brown.

125

LILLIAN: You are not my father. This isn't mine, take it. My Father's name is William Dickenson.

ROBERT: No, keep it Lillian it's yours, I want you to have it.

MARGARITE: Lillian . . . Who's at the door?

LILLIAN: Mommy come quick, it's some man trying to be Daddy.

MARGARITE: *(goes to the door, and becomes highly agitated at seeing her former husband Robert standing in her doorway)* Lillian, give me this box. We don't accept things from strangers, and go to your room and finish your homework. *(raising her voice and shaking the box in Robert's face)* What are you doing here? Why are you here? I don't need you coming around. Don't you get it? I want you out of my life. You've got some nerve coming here, what are you trying to do, disrupt our lives? *(she shoves the box at Robert)* Take this junk and get lost. How did you even find me?

ROBERT: But Margarite . . .

MARGARITE: *(very sarcastic, standing with hands on her hips)* But what? You saw the child that answered the door, she was your daughter, years ago, but not now.

ROBERT: Was, what do you mean, was? She still is.

MARGARITE: That's what I said, was . . . you're not deaf. Lillian was seven months old when we divorced, or have you forgotten? You didn't bother to come around to see her, so why start now? You were no good then and you will never be any good to her, me, or anyone else for that matter, not now, and you're a disgrace.

ROBERT: *(sincerely pleading)* But! Margarite! I'm a changed man now.

MARGARITE: Changed! Changed! Well honey, you are many years too late. You should have thought about being changed when you laid your hands on me, before and after Lillian's birth. She doesn't know you and she never will. I don't want to see your face around here again. You're a poor excuse for a father and a man.

ROBERT: Margarite . . . Please give me one last chance?

MARGARITE: Give you what? Do I look crazy to you? You've got to be out of your mind. You had plenty of chances and you blew every last one. Lillian's dad has died, the only father she has known, and as far as you're concerned I am her only blood relative. As long as I'm on this earth, she will never know you.

ROBERT: Margarite, please . . .

MARGARITE: Get lost Robert Brown, stay out of our lives. If you ever show your face around here again, I will call the police and make sure they put you in jail forever . . . understand? Goodbye. *(slams door in Robert's face)* I'm tired.

LILLIAN: *(enters living room, hugs her Mom)* Mommy is everything okay?

MARGARITE: Yes Sweetheart. I'm going to call Zera and Jahad today to see if they feel up to going to Disney World.

LILLIAN: Really Mommy?

MARGARITE: *(hugs Lillian)* Yes, sweetheart this is something we all need, and we are going to do it together.

THE END

9 781964 037882